'Explain yourself, sir,' snapped the unctuous voice of the celebrant, and Olivia saw Gregor blink slowly, almost as if he needed to close his eyes to break the link between them.

Not that it worked.

As soon as he lifted those thick dark lashes the connection was made again, and it seemed as if neither of them could look away.

Despite the distance between the opposite ends of the aisle she could see the shadows in his eyes, and saw too the way his chest expanded with the steadying breath he drew in before he spoke the unavoidable words.

'This ceremony cannot continue because the lady is already married—to me.'

There was utter silence for several seconds, before pandemonium erupted around her. It seemed as if every single one of the guests had something to say about the shocking turn of events, but Olivia found it hard to care—not when her overloaded emotions were finally giving up under the accumulated strain of two devastating years.

The last thing she saw before her knees refused to support her any further and the darkness overwhelmed her was Gregor's arms reaching towards her, the helpless frustration in his eyes telling her better than words that *he* wanted to be the one to catch her as she fell.

Josie Metcalfe lives in Cornwall with her long-suffering husband. They have four children. When she was an army brat, frequently on the move, books became the only friends that came with her wherever she went. Now that she writes them herself she is making new friends, and hates saying goodbye at the end of a book—but there are always more characters in her head, clamouring for attention until she can't wait to tell their stories.

Recent titles by the same author:

A FAMILY FOR HIS TINY TWINS*
A WIFE FOR THE BABY DOCTOR*
SHEIKH SURGEON CLAIMS HIS BRIDE†
THE DOCTOR'S BRIDE BY SUNRISE†
TWINS FOR A CHRISTMAS BRIDE
A MARRIAGE MEANT TO BE

*Neonatal duet
†*Brides of Penhally Bay*

HER LONG-LOST HUSBAND

BY
JOSIE METCALFE

First published in Great Britain 2010
Large Print edition 2010
Harlequin Mills & Boon Limited,
Eton House, 18-24 Paradise Road,
Richmond, Surrey TW9 1SR

ISBN: 978 0 263 21124 5

Harlequin Mills & Boon policy is to use papers that are
natural, renewable and recyclable products and made
from wood grown in sustainable forests. The logging and
manufacturing process conform to the legal environmental
regulations of the country of origin.

Printed and bound in Great Britain
by CPI Antony Rowe, Chippenham, Wiltshire

HER LONG-LOST
HUSBAND

PROLOGUE

'THANK you,' Gregor said distractedly, grateful that the usher had come to hold the door open for him when he'd struggled with the weight of it, but he barely heard his own words over the frantic beating of his heart.

He'd been so afraid that he'd arrive too late, and even now as his eyes adjusted to the comparative gloom inside the church, the familiar traditional organ music died away and he heard the sonorous tones of the celebrant echoing over the heads of the couple standing before the altar.

'*Dearly beloved...*'

The first words silenced the soft sibilance of whispers as the whole congregation concentrated on the time-hallowed words.

'*We are gathered...*' This time they would probably *all* be gathered in the serried ranks of pews, he thought wryly, her genteel collection of Mannington-Forbes uncles, aunts and cousins on one side, all with that noticeably supercilious air that seemed to come with a hint of blue blood. The groom's side, too, would be filled with the overfed scions of old money and even older titles, with long thin noses and barely a normal jawbone between them.

Not that he bothered to spare a look for any of them.

The only person who filled his gaze was the slender wraith of a woman whose delicate ivory dress made her seem almost as insubstantial as dandelion fluff...a far cry from the fun-filled, captivating woman he'd once known.

Even from this distance he could see how much she'd changed, the differences even more obvious in person than they'd been in that artfully posed studio portrait he'd seen just this morning, but were the changes all physical? Was there anything left of the joyous, passionate woman whom he had once known? '*...any reason why they should not be married, let him speak now or for ever hold his peace.*'

The words were obviously spoken by rote, a challenge that was thrown out at every such ceremony with little expectation that anyone would ever stand up to make a declaration.

Well, no-one would be standing up this time, either, but only because he was completely incapable of getting out of his wheelchair unaided. That didn't mean that the objection wouldn't be made. He had no alternative, so he drew in a sharp breath.

'This ceremony cannot continue,' he announced, surprised by the way the acoustics in the vaulted space seemed to magnify the words until it almost sounded as if he'd shouted.

Perhaps he had. It was difficult to be certain while he was in such turmoil. All he knew was that his heart was beating so fast that it was shaking his whole body while he waited to see what would happen, and his eyes never left the slender figure at the foot of the altar steps.

The congregation's response reminded him of the time he'd seen a hive of bees disturbed but, of course, these were very upper-crust bees that did little more than gasp and glare in the direction of the intruder; bees whose mutters and murmurs were easily subdued by the celebrant's testy demand.

'Why should I stop this ceremony? On what grounds?'

He'd been focusing on that slender back and knew from her sudden unnatural stillness that she must have recognised his voice.

He regretted the fact that things had happened this way. It had been sheer chance that had put that magazine article in his hands this morning or he would never have known what was happening until it had been too late. Obviously, it would have been so much better if he'd had time to contact her earlier, then she would have been saved this embarrassment.

As it was he was left sitting there, his eyes almost dazzled by the rainbow of colours thrown across the skirt of her delicate dress by the sun pouring through the stained-glass windows. Then, moving as slowly and stiffly as though she were a mechanical automaton, she turned to stare at him, wide-eyed with a mixture of shock and disbelief.

There was a strange ringing sound in Olivia's ears. Unfortunately, it was nothing like the joyous peal that was due to sound from the bell-tower at the end of the ceremony.

And that voice!

The unforgettable husky edge to it and the so-sexy hint of an accent that had always been able to turn her knees to water, right from the very first time she'd met him.

It could only be Gregor's voice.

But that was impossible.

Gregor was dead.

She shuddered with the dreadful finality of that thought, and guilt flooded through her anew that she would never be able to forget the first man…the *only* man…she'd ever loved.

Was it guilt that had her imagining that she could still hear his voice; guilt that she was even *trying* to pretend that she was over her loss?

She hadn't needed to turn around to know that Gregor wouldn't be there. She had done just that so many times before when wishful thinking had had her convinced that she could hear him. She'd lost count of the number of times she'd thought that she recognised him in some tall dark-haired man with an almost impatient stride and quick-silver eyes.

But in the end she couldn't resist turning to look.

In spite of the fact that she'd been standing beside Ashley, the man her mother had always intended as the ideal husband for her stubborn daughter, she hadn't been able to stop herself turning to look back down the length of the flower-decked aisle.

Her breath caught in her throat and her heart nearly stopped beating altogether when she didn't find Gregor standing there as lean and powerful as the day she'd last seen him, but seated in a wheelchair with those unearthly pale eyes sunk into a face that was a mere shadow of the handsome man she'd once known.

It *was* Gregor.

He was alive!

Alive, but…dear God, he looked dreadful! So pale and grey and…

Was he sick? Dying?

Had the confirmation of his death just been premature? He certainly wore the strained look of someone who'd been enduring severe pain—mental or physical—for a very long time.

Dimly she was aware that there were muttering voices all around her, but they were as inconsequential as the hum of bees in a summer flowerbed when it felt as if her heart would stop beating with the culmination of two years of agony.

Those eyes!

As vulnerable as he looked now, the life in Gregor's eyes had always seared her with its intensity; had drawn her to him as fiercely as the most powerful magnet. And when she realised that she was helpless to look away from him, Olivia knew that hadn't changed, even though it had been so long since she'd last seen him; even though she'd tried to convince herself that she'd come to terms with his final disappearance from her life.

'Explain yourself, sir,' snapped the unctuous voice of the celebrant, and Olivia saw Gregor blink slowly, almost as if he needed to close his eyes to break the link between them.

Not that it worked.

As soon as he lifted those thick dark lashes the connection was made again and it seemed as if neither of them could look away.

She suddenly seemed to be aware of everything about him…the way he straightened his shoulders inside the jacket he wore…the way the jacket almost seemed too small on him, as if he'd had to borrow it to be here...the stark contrast of the trousers that only seemed to exaggerate the extreme thinness of his thighs as he sat there passively in the chair.

Despite the distance between the opposite ends of the aisle she could see the shadows in his eyes and saw, too, the way his chest expanded with the steadying breath he drew in before he spoke the unavoidable words.

'This ceremony cannot continue because the lady is already married—to me.'

There was utter silence for several seconds before pandemonium erupted around her. It seemed as if every single one of the guests had something to say about the shocking turn of events, but Olivia found it hard to care, not when her overloaded emotions were finally giving up under the accumulated strain of two devastating years.

The last thing she saw before her knees refused to support her any further and the darkness overwhelmed her was Gregor's arms reaching towards her, the helpless frustration in his eyes telling her better than words that *he* wanted to be the one to catch her as she fell.

CHAPTER ONE

'OLIVIA!'

That sharp voice was her mother's, piercing through the cotton-wool that filled Olivia's head and letting in the cacophony that surrounded her. She'd had so many years of hearing that mixture of exasperation and disappointment that she'd grown all-too adept at shutting it out.

This time was no different as she opted for keeping her eyes closed for just a moment or two longer while she gathered up the fortitude to face the storm breaking over her head. She would bet good money that her father would be nowhere to be found. Sometimes she'd wondered if he was merely a figment of her imagination, she'd seen so little of him during her childhood. There was little doubt that her mother had married him for his bank balance rather than his quiet love of the nature contained within the family estate, and it had always been obvious to Olivia, once she'd grown up enough to notice such things, that he eminently preferred the company of his dogs to that of his wife.

'Is it *true*?' That sharply demanding hiss—just too loud to be called a whisper—was Ashley's mother. Only Phyllida Grayson-Smythe could sound *that* outraged *that* quietly, especially when the two things most precious to her might be hurt…the family name and her darling son's feelings.

'Of course not, Mother.' That was Ash's usual placating tone as he soothed his domineering mother. If the woman ever found out the real reason why the two of them had agreed to this wedding… 'Olivia's marriage ended when her husband was declared dead.'

'Except I'm obviously not dead,' said the slightly husky voice with the so-sexy hint of an accent that haunted her dreams, and Olivia finally forced herself to open her eyes, still not convinced that this wasn't just another of the nightmares that had returned with a vengeance ever since she'd given in to the incessant pressure and agreed to marry Ashley.

It took only a second or two to discover that she was lying full-length on the scarlet carpet at the foot of the altar steps, totally surrounded by what seemed to be every single one of the hundreds of guests.

So, how was it possible that the first pair of eyes she met were Gregor's, their silvery gleam darkened to pewter by concern?

'Are you all right?' It was impossible to actually hear his softly spoken question but it was so easy to read his lips, especially when she didn't seem able to drag her eyes away from him.

Was she all right? She hardly knew with so many emotions whirling around inside her, fighting for space with all the questions she longed to ask.

What was the matter with him?

Why was he in a wheelchair?

How sick was he?

Was his illness the reason he hadn't come back to her after his last deployment?

Had the report of his death been concocted because he hadn't *wanted* to come back?

Had he simply fallen out of love with her?

Had he just not cared that her heart had been broken?

Embarrassment at her current predicament and the fact that there would be no way of avoiding seeing highly coloured accounts of today's events reported in the media seemed unimportant against the more fundamental emotions trying to wrench her apart.

Finally, there were only two that really mattered—her overwhelming joy that the man she loved was still alive, and a growing anger that he could have treated her so heartlessly.

'Let me up,' she demanded, slapping impatiently at Ash's hands when he would have prevented her from extricating herself from such a vulnerable position.

'Are you sure you should?' her erstwhile groom cautioned.

'Of course I'm sure.' It was an effort when she was quivering in every muscle, but she kept her voice firm. 'I fainted from shock, not because I'm ill,' she added, glad that she wasn't having to fight with her mother's choice of a vast billowing meringue of a dress as she scrambled to her feet.

'But, Olivia… Darling!'

She could almost hear her mother's brain scrambling to find some innocuous explanation for this whole fiasco…some way of saving face in front of all these eminent people…but Olivia suddenly knew that there was only one possible course of action.

'Ladies and gentlemen,' she began, deliberately ignoring the fact that there was a liberal sprinkling of titled relatives among the throng. 'As you will no doubt have realised, there will not be a wedding ceremony today. There is, however, a reception ready and waiting, so those of you who have been looking forward to the day so that they can catch up with far-flung friends and relations are welcome to make their way there.'

She concentrated hard on keeping a smile pinned to her face and trying to meet as many eyes as possible in the hope that she could fool everyone into believing that she was completely calm and in control.

Out of the corner of her eye she caught a glimpse of her mother's frantic gestures but deliberately ignored them to add, 'I hope you all have a wonderful time and…and that you will raise a glass in thanksgiving that Gregor's life has been spared. Thank you all for coming today.'

She would have loved to have been able to walk away at that point to find somewhere peaceful to regain her composure, but even thinking about putting one foot in front of the other was beyond her, especially with Gregor watching her every move.

'Olivia?' Ashley wrapped a supportive arm around her, but instead of feeling comforted, she felt smothered and…and guilty. 'Is there anything I can do?' he muttered close to her ear. 'Shall I get rid of him?'

The sudden heat in Gregor's gaze was enough to tell her that if there was any 'getting rid of' to be done, it wouldn't be Ashley doing it.

The recognition of that should have been ridiculous, especially with one man in good health and the other apparently unable to manoeuvre without a wheelchair.

'No, thank you, Ashley. That won't be necessary,' she said distantly, as though the man hadn't been stood beside her just a few minutes ago waiting to exchange their marriage vows.

'Well, do you want me to take you some-where?' he offered, muttering under the cover of the surrounding hubbub. 'The limousine is waiting outside. Where would you like to go?'

Olivia pondered briefly, for just one moment tempted to take to her heels and ask the limousine driver to find somewhere far away where she could bury herself while she put her shattered feelings together, but then realised that it would be an impossibility until she spoke to Gregor; until she found out where he had been for the past two years and what was the matter with him that he'd had to make his appearance today in a wheelchair.

A quick glance around the stately old building told her what she needed to know before she de-liberately met Gregor's gaze, then flicked her eyes towards the heavy wooden door beside the Lady Chapel at the side of the church for several seconds.

She saw him glance across then back again to meet her eyes. A single nod confirmed that he had understood, and a briefly raised hand showing all five fingers told her that he would meet her at the side exit in five minutes. Only then did she turn her attention to Ashley.

'Ash, can I borrow the car?' she asked softly, careful not to let either of the mothers overhear.

'Borrow it?' He smiled down at her indulgently, effortlessly putting on the appearance of the besotted husband-to-be, the way he had throughout the months of preparation that had led up to this day. 'Parker's at our disposal for the whole of the day, remember? Where do you want to go? Not back to your mother's, I bet, not with the reception set up in the Great Hall. Nor my parents' pile,' he continued with a grimace before adding, softly, 'I know...I could take you to the penthouse flat. I doubt anyone would look for us there.'

The penthouse flat was bigger than most four-bedroom houses and took up the whole top floor of the city building that housed the top-flight investment business the Grayson-Smythes had been running for the past century or more. Of course, as the sole heir, Ash was welcome to use the apartment whenever he wanted to spend some time in London.

'Going to the penthouse would be a good idea, Ash. The building has state-of-the-art security, in case the press try to follow you. But what I wanted was to borrow the car for myself. It's probably going to be the only vehicle immediately available that Gregor's wheelchair will fit into, and we'll need to get going quickly if we don't want the paparazzi hounding us.'

For a moment Ashley was as speechless as if she'd winded him, his hazel eyes wide with disbelief.

'You're going to…to go off with him?' he demanded hoarsely, and she was certain that only rigorous training from childhood kept him from shouting the question.

'Of course I am,' she said steadily, determined to sound calm. 'I was told he was dead when he obviously isn't, so I need to talk to Gregor…preferably without several dozen people hanging around us. I need to find out where he's been…and also whether we're still legally married. Until I know those answers I won't be able to decide what happens next. I certainly have no desire to be a bigamist. Neither of our families would ever forgive me for that sort of impropriety.'

Ashley did his best to dissuade her, becoming quite heated as the last of the congregation was

ushered firmly out of the church, but Olivia stuck
to her guns. It wasn't difficult, as part of her attention was taken up with trying to keep sight of
Gregor as he made his way around the far side
of the church.

After two years without seeing him…of believing that she would never see him again…it
was impossible not to give in to the temptation
to feast her eyes on him.

She was fascinated to see that he somehow
seemed to be able to keep to the shadows and
move unobtrusively, in spite of the fact he was
using something as noticeable as a wheelchair.

'Ash, *please*,' Olivia said, and the determined
tone of her voice finally stopped her handsome
would-be-groom in mid-argument so that she
could continue more discreetly. 'We both know
the reason why we were getting married, so
there's no need for you to play the broken-
hearted lover—especially not with me.'

He sighed heavily then capitulated with almost
juvenile bad grace, just as she'd known he would.

'So, what do you want me to do? Escort the
two of you out to the car and wave you off with
my blessings?'

'Hardly!' She shuddered at the thought. The photographers inevitable at any sort of society wedding would go into the sort of feeding frenzy that would plaster their pictures across every tabloid newspaper in the country and take weeks to subside. 'Can you get the car sent around to the side exit?' She gestured discreetly to the dark solid wood door at the other side of the church and was surprised that Gregor seemed to have completely disappeared.

Panic made her heart give an extra hollow thump.

Had he grown tired of waiting? He never had been a particularly patient person. If something needed doing, he'd always been the one to dive straight in and get the job done as quickly and as efficiently as possible. Had she missed her chance to ask him where he'd been and why?

'You just want me to send it round to pick the two of you up?'

'If you're feeling particularly brave, you could do your best to stop my mother setting off in pursuit,' she suggested, and he shook his head with an expression of horror.

'No way! And whatever happens, Olivia, don't tell me where you're going, then she can't torture it out of me,' he begged, teasingly, then grew serious again. 'Keep in touch, please…at least to let me know you're all right.'

'I will, Ash, and…well, I'm sorry things turned out this way for you.' She put her hand on the expensive fabric of his sleeve and gave his arm a squeeze. 'If I'd had any idea that Gregor was still alive, I'd never have let my mother bully me into…'

'Hey, don't worry about it,' he said as an unholy gleam lit his hazel eyes. 'Just think what a wonderfully tragic figure I'll make as I struggle on bravely in spite of my broken heart.'

'Idiot!' She slapped his arm and pushed him away. 'You'd better go and organise that car or I'll break something other than your heart,' she warned, then set off across the nave without a backward glance, hurrying towards the shadowy recess where Gregor had disappeared.

By the time Olivia finally joined him by the side door, Gregor had decided that he hated the scent of lilies.

The church was absolutely filled with fabulous arrangements of them, each creamy blossom nearly the size of a dinner plate with burgundy freckles shading the throat, but they had been the thing on which he'd deliberately focused his attention while Olivia talked to the floppy-haired clothes horse she'd been about to marry.

He reached out to open the side door a crack in an attempt to dispel the heavy perfume, only to have it replaced by the familiar cinnamon scent of the woman who was suddenly standing close beside him.

'So, where are we going?' he growled as his back complained that it had been far too long since his last lot of analgesics. But, then, he'd been far too busy worrying that he wouldn't arrive at the church in time to realise that he'd missed a dose. It seemed as if he'd been living in his own private version of hell for ever, and it obviously wasn't over, yet.

'I haven't thought that far ahead,' she admitted, then added pointedly, 'After all, until a few minutes ago, I had no idea you were still alive, let alone that you were going to turn up in the middle of my wedding.'

For the first time in a very long time, Gregor actually found himself struggling not to grin. So, his feisty Livvy *was* still in there, ready and willing to fight back. Her mother hadn't completely managed to get her daughter under her upper-crust thumb once he was out of the picture.

'Is there a hotel nearby, where we could talk?' he suggested, all too aware that he needed to get his next set of tablets inside him as soon as possible. The last thing he wanted was to collapse into a gibbering wreck before he'd had a chance to explain what had happened over the last two years.

'Several, but nowhere that I could guarantee the staff and guests wouldn't take the chance of earning some easy money by alerting the newshounds,' she warned. 'All three of the better ones in the immediate area have wedding guests staying there, so there's no chance we would be anonymous.'

A gleaming black limousine purred to a halt the other side of the neatly clipped holly hedge and when the chauffeur lost no time in hurrying round to open the back door wide, Gregor rolled his eyes that he hadn't anticipated that their transport was likely to be something as over-the-top as this.

It was almost comical to see the way the smartly dressed driver's face fell when he first caught sight of the wheelchair and realised that there was no way that they were going to be able to get it into the vehicle, spacious as it was.

Gregor took pity on him. 'If you open up the front passenger door, I can transfer out of this,' he said, tapping the rim of one wheel. 'The chair will then fold flat,' he added, as ever having to tamp down his impatience that he was so dependent on other people for such simple things.

Then there was the fact that he hadn't wanted Livvy to see him in such a pathetic state; to see him having to laboriously heave himself out of the chair when all he could rely on was his upper-body strength.

He hardly dared to look at her for fear he would see dismay…even revulsion at his weakness. He'd never been obsessed with the way his body looked—couldn't be bothered wasting precious time pumping iron in a gym—but at least, before, he'd been strong enough to intermittently indulge in the romantic gesture of sweeping Livvy off her feet. At this precise moment he was so shaky with the combination of pain and overwrought emotion that he could barely sit upright to look her in the eye.

As soon as he'd settled himself into the butter-soft leather seat, the chauffeur whisked the chair away towards the back of the vehicle, stowing it away as swiftly as though it was something he did on a daily basis.

'Can you help me?' Livvy asked, startling him by speaking almost in his ear from inside the back of the car. 'I can't reach the zip.'

He nearly whiplashed his neck turning to see what she was doing, for one mind-boggling second imagining that she intended stripping off in broad daylight.

No such luck, he mourned when he saw that she'd pulled a sweater on over her head and was trying to loosen the tightly fitted top to her dress—was it called a basque, or something similar?—so that she could remove it. She'd already pulled on a pair of indigo jeans under the skirt, the casual outfit obviously retrieved from the suitcases that must have been stowed in the car in readiness for the newly married couple's departure on their honeymoon.

He cursed silently when he realised that his

fingers were visibly trembling as he gripped the tiny tab. He tried to tell himself that it was simply because this was the closest he'd been to a woman since…well, who knew how long? He honestly couldn't remember when he'd last helped a woman to take her clothes off. Unfortunately, the tremor was rather more likely to be a result of the frustrating weakness that plagued him, exacerbated by the battery of tests he'd undergone over the last couple of days. Until the specialist was able to give him some sort of reassurance that there was a surgical solution to his problem, he'd decided to delay letting Olivia know of his return…only to have his decision reversed, his hand forced this morning by the sight of that heart-stopping photo.

'Thank you.' The unexpectedly husky sound of her voice suddenly made him realise that he was still gripping the edge of the fabric even though the fastener was open, with his eyes fixed blindly on the sensuous curve of silky skin that he'd revealed.

It was pale creamy skin with the slightest natural olive tint that always made it look as if it carried a lingering hint of summer sun even in the depths of winter; skin that felt even softer to the touch of his fingertips than the secret silken fabrics she loved to wear against it.

Just the thought of touching…of exploring to see if her body still felt the same when he ran his hands over it, had his own body reacting in a purely masculine way for the first time since…

'Gregor?' The tone of her voice told him it wasn't the first time she'd called his name, but when his eyes flicked up to meet hers and he saw how darkly dilated the pupils were, he was too elated by the evidence that she was equally affected by their proximity to care.

'So, where are we going, then?' asked the chauffeur as he opened the door and slid into his seat and the thread of awareness that had been spinning out between the two of them, re-establishing the connection that had been severed in a split second nearly two years ago, was snapped in an instant.

CHAPTER TWO

'WE CERTAINLY can't turn up at my mother's,' Olivia said with feeling. 'Not with the reception set up there.'

She couldn't help a wry grin when both the men in the front of the vehicle laughed. Gregor had never needed very long to get on the same wavelength with other men when he wanted to, and 'just-call-me-Parker' the chauffeur was no different.

'And I can't see you being very welcome at the Grayson-Smythes' elegant abode,' Parker offered, sounding more than a little tongue-in-cheek.

'Nor their son's penthouse,' Gregor added, and, along with her shock at discovering that he must have been lip-reading her conversation with Ash, Olivia found herself half-hoping that there was a hint of jealousy in his tone. Then she gave herself a mental slap for the thought because there was absolutely no reason for him to feel any jealousy.

Not that he would. After all, the fact that he was alive today must mean that he'd intended disappearing out of her life two years ago, and added to that, there was the detail that he'd done it without a word of warning…

'I expect you sold our place,' he said, and the fact that it obviously wasn't voiced as a question nettled her for some reason.

'Why would I have?' she retorted sharply. 'It's my home.'

It was also the place that was filled with the echoes of all the happy memories of the two of them; memories formed in the days when she'd naïvely believed that they'd be together for ever.

She was almost certain that she'd heard him mutter '*our* home' under his breath, but it wasn't worth a fight to argue the matter, especially in front of an audience.

Anyway, Gregor wouldn't be staying in what had once been their home for any longer than it took for him to tell her where he'd been for the last two years. Once she knew why he'd just disappeared out of her life like that, she could instruct the family's solicitor to sort out the confusion about his death then draw up the necessary papers to end their marriage...properly and legally this time.

Although whether she'd ever have the strength to go through all the interminable preparations for a rescheduled wedding with Ash was another matter, considering that she hadn't really wanted to marry him in the first place.

She was vaguely aware that Gregor was giving Parker directions to the flat in the renovated Edwardian town house, but her thoughts were definitely elsewhere.

Now that she had time to take stock of her reaction to the events of the last hour, she would have to admit that her overwhelming feeling was one of relief.

She'd never felt anything beyond a slightly detached friendship towards Ashley, heir to the stately pile and its countless acres of beautiful countryside that was almost within sight of her own childhood home. But when her mother's campaign for Olivia to do her duty for the continuation of the Mannington-Forbes into the next generation had become totally unbearable, she'd enlisted her one-time neighbour to concoct their little scheme.

The fact that he'd been under very similar pressure from his own family—and had been equally averse to the idea of any sort of romantic attachment—had been the only reasons why she'd allowed herself to be distracted from her determination to concentrate her energies totally on her career.

So, what was going to happen now?

Obviously, she and Gregor were going to have to talk, but what then?

Once he'd told her where he'd been for the last two years and why he hadn't told her he was going to leave her like that—without a word— *would* she be calmly making an appointment with the Mannington-Forbes' family solicitor to draw up the papers necessary to set a divorce in—?

'Are you going to need a hand?' asked Parker, and Olivia suddenly realised that he'd stopped the limousine right outside the front of the elegant Edwardian building that housed her…their…flat.

'Yes, please—' she began, only to be interrupted by Gregor.

'Not necessary, thanks,' he said gruffly. 'If you get the chair, I can manage the rest.'

Olivia pressed her lips together to stop the denial that wanted to emerge, knowing that the stubborn man she'd married wouldn't welcome her interference. If he said he could manage…

But it must have been obvious, even to the chauffeur's untrained eye, that Gregor was in a bad way. His skin was quite grey, and there was a sheen of sweat over it that told her he was definitely in a great deal of pain. Not that he would ever willingly admit to any weakness. That had been one of the first things she'd learned about him, long before she'd discovered what had made him that way.

She slid across the buttery-soft leather of the back seat and stepped out into the nip of the overcast day, glad she'd changed into something more suitable than the one-of-a-kind designer wedding dress now lying on the back seat, abandoned without a single qualm.

Trying to concentrate on getting the rest of her own belongings out of the back of the vehicle, she found herself deliberately positioning herself where she could keep an eye on what Gregor was doing without him being able to see that she was watching over him.

'Miss? Are you *sure* he can manage? There must be dozens of stairs inside that place,' Parker muttered out of the side of his mouth when he hurried back to help her with the set of perfectly matched luggage her mother had insisted on supplying for the honeymoon.

'He'll manage,' she reassured the man. *Even if it kills him*, she added silently, knowing that, in spite of the fact that he was in a wheelchair, there was little chance that the intervening two years would have done anything to lessen Gregor's fiercely independent streak. 'When the house was converted into flats they installed a beautiful old Edwardian lift, rescued from another building that was being demolished. So, neither of us will have to struggle with stairs.'

'Well, if you're sure…' He cast a worried glance to where Gregor had doggedly manoeuvred the chair across the pavement and up the beautifully restored Minton tiling of the front path towards the access ramp that had been installed not long after they'd bought their flat.

'I'm sure,' she reassured him, warmed by his

obvious concern. 'Anyway, you probably need to get back to the reception, in case any of the more decrepit aunts and uncles need ferrying about. Don't worry about us,' she reassured him. 'We'll be fine as long as the paparazzi piranhas don't find out where we've gone.'

'Well, they won't find out from me,' he said stoutly as he took charge of the largest case, then grinned back at her over his shoulder as he set off in Gregor's wake. 'If anyone should ask me, I can't tell them what I don't know. After all, when I dropped the two of you off at the airport, you didn't tell me where you were going. For all I know, you were going to take advantage of the honeymoon booking.'

Olivia smiled at the thought of all those journalists milling around the international departure lounge at Heathrow airport, trying to find her. She was just sending up a silent prayer that some film star or pop idol would do something particularly idiotic to take the spotlight off her own life when she turned the corner in the corridor and saw Gregor waiting by the lift.

Suddenly she remembered that the old-fashioned concertina-style doors weren't the easiest thing to cope with when you were upright. They would be nearly impossible for someone hampered by a cumbersome wheel-chair. She only had to see the exhausted expression on his face to know that Gregor had finally reached the limits of his capabilities, and that was something she'd never seen before.

'Would you like a cup of tea before you start your journey back?' Olivia offered the chauffeur as he stacked the luggage to one side of the creaking cubicle, the turmoil of her thoughts suddenly making her want to cling to this relative stranger to put off the moment that she would be alone with the silent man sharing the limited space in the lift.

For one awful moment she nearly doubled over with pain at the thought that Gregor only wanted to speak to her to confirm that he wanted to set their divorce in motion. How stupid was it that the simple thought could affect her so strongly? She'd actually believed that she'd moved so far beyond their fractured marriage that she'd been just seconds from making her vows to another man.

But then, in spite of the fact that she'd been in-telligent enough to virtually sail through her medical training, she was obviously crazy enough to harbour more than a lingering regard for the man she'd once loved beyond life itself. In fact, just the thought that this might be the last time she ever saw him...once he obtained her agreement to the legal ending of their vows...made her feel as though a giant hand was clenching tighter and tighter around her heart.

'That's a very kind thought, miss, but my wife always sends me off with a flask on days when she knows I'm going to be doing a lot of hanging around. Anyway, I don't like to take the risk of getting a parking ticket out on the road, there. For some reason, those jobsworths in charge of policing the yellow lines seem to make a beeline for any car that's a bit out of the ordinary...and that swanky limousine is definitely something out of the ordinary.'

Olivia was absurdly grateful for the man's conversation, otherwise she was convinced that she and Gregor would have made the journey up to the third floor in complete silence.

In fact, now that she thought about it, he hadn't said a single word to her since the decision about their destination had been made.

'Are you sure about that tea?' she asked when the cases were stacked neatly inside the hallway of the flat, uncomfortably aware just how much she wanted the kindly older man to stay. Suddenly, there was such an uncomfortable tension filling the air between Gregor and herself that every nerve seemed stretched tight enough to vibrate audibly.

'No, thanks, miss. I'll be off, now, to avoid the traffic.' He paused for a moment in the doorway, his forehead pleated in a worried frown as he looked from one to the other. 'Take care of yourselves, and…and good luck, to both of you,' he blurted, then pulled the door closed hurriedly behind him.

Olivia shivered, although she wasn't cold. The click of the door catch echoed around the flat and sounded strangely as if the two of them had just been locked in together, like prison inmates forced to share a cell.

It was such a crazy idea that she wondered if her brain had been scrambled by the events of the day and their inevitable consequences.

Logically, she knew that this was nothing more than a flat; the one they'd hunted for and chosen together; the place that had once been their refuge from the world…until the day Gregor had walked out, the way he'd always done at the start of his next deployment, and had disappeared out of her life, presumed dead.

It always circled back to that, didn't it; to the glaring fact that Gregor hadn't died; to the maelstrom of thoughts and feelings that left her unable to voice the questions that most needed answering.

Had he simply decided not to return? Or was it his injuries that had made him abandon her? She could easily imagine his pride preventing him from coming back if it meant he would be a burden on her.

Or was it simply that he just didn't love her any more? Had it only been the fact that she was in danger of committing bigamy that had brought him out of hiding? If so, he could certainly have chosen his moment with a little more consideration for Ash's and her family's social standing, to say nothing of her own shock and embarrassment.

That thought was enough to summon up enough resentment to bolster her to face him, but when she turned, the expression she saw on his face was so desolate that the sharp words she'd been framing caught in her throat and robbed her of the power to speak.

Silently, he was looking around him, his eyes travelling hungrily over every single item in the room as though he'd actually missed seeing them.

Suddenly, for the first time since he'd disappeared from her life, she was glad she'd altered so little in what had been their home, rather than feeling half-ashamed that she couldn't bear to get rid of the things they'd chosen together.

'Can…?' She had to pause to clear her throat before she could continue, emotion suddenly clogging her throat. 'Can I get you anything, Gregor? When did you last eat?'

For a moment, it didn't matter why he'd stayed away; why he'd left her believing that he was dead. All she could think was that he looked so ill that all she wanted to do was wrap him in her arms and take care of him until he was well again.

'I need some water to take my tablets… please.' There was a reedy note of desperation in his voice that made her medically-tuned antennae vibrate a warning. Gregor hated taking any sort of medication. He wasn't the kind of man to give in to any kind of weakness, if he could help it, so whatever had put him in the wheelchair and left him this eager to take pills must be serious.

'Water,' she repeated blankly, feeling more and more sick as the possible diagnoses running through her head grew more and more dire.

By the time she returned with a brimming glass he had a container of prescription drugs in his hand but seemed almost incapable of dealing with the child-proof cap.

Silently she held out the glass, forcing him to take it so that he couldn't avoid letting her deal with the container.

'How many?' she asked, her tension increasing exponentially when she read the label and saw just how heavy-duty the painkillers were.

'Two,' he said gruffly, and her concern rose still higher when she saw how eagerly he swallowed them down.

'You should have something to eat with those, unless you want them to make holes in your stomach lining. What would you like—soup and toast, or something more substantial?'

Not that she could remember what was left in her freezer. She'd been working right up to the last minute, yesterday, her shift in A and E running over…the way it usually did…and just hadn't had the time to do anything more than bequeath the perishables from her fridge to one of the neighbours. As for organising to put the flat on the market… Somehow, in spite of her mother's frequent reminders, she just hadn't been able to force herself to come to terms with the idea of selling it yet.

'Livvy…when are you going to stand still long enough to draw breath?' Gregor said softly, and stopped her in her tracks, her scurrying thoughts scattered to the four winds.

How many times had he said exactly those words to her during her training, only to steal what little breath she had with the sweetest, most caring of kisses?

Not that his kisses had stayed sweet and caring; at least, not for long when the emotions between them had ignited into the sort of inferno that had vaporised the rest of the world and left the two of them as the sole survivors in a new and magical land.

'Gregor…' Did her voice sound as shaky as it felt as she turned to face him?

His colour was no better…well, it wouldn't be. The tablets hadn't had time to be absorbed into his system yet. And his hair was too long…much longer than the length he preferred it, to keep the tendency to curl under control. And were those grey hairs gleaming at his temples? There certainly hadn't been any there the last time she'd seen him.

And his eyes…

Those liquid-silver depths had always held secrets, but that was hardly surprising, considering the things he'd gone through as a child and those he dealt with on a daily basis with each deployment to one of the world's trouble spots. Only, now there was something else…a glimpse into something that sent a shiver through her before he deliberately blinked and shut her out.

'Are you going to sit down and talk with me?' he asked, and there was a definite challenge in his words; a challenge that, after two years of thinking he was dead, she suddenly found herself resisting.

'I'll sit down and talk when I've made us both something to eat,' she announced firmly as she turned back towards the kitchen. 'I haven't eaten since stupid-o'clock this morning, and you look as if you haven't eaten since some time in the last millennium, to say nothing of needing to take something with those drugs.'

And those drugs and his need to take them were going to be one of the first things on the agenda when they started talking, she decided as her medical brain started working again. That strength of prescription was usually only administered to in-patients under medical supervision, often in the first few hours or days post-operatively...or to patients in the final stages of terminal cancer, a vicious little voice reminded her, even though she tried to refuse to listen.

She could almost hear Gregor fuming behind her as she retrieved some home-made soup from the freezer and transferred it to the microwave, and for the first time that day she actually felt like chuckling aloud.

In the two years since he'd disappeared, she'd found herself mentally putting him on a pedestal, ignoring his all-too-human flaws to remember only the many good points in his character. It was so good to have the fact that he'd never been a saintly person brought home to her like this.

He never *had* liked being thwarted. Once he'd

decided on a course of action, each separate sphere within his military and his medical training had ensured that he would do his utmost to achieve his goal. For just a moment, it felt as if there was a degree of poetic justice in that she finally had the power to exert *her* will.

Of course, that thought immediately made her feel guilty, because what sort of a person was she to take pleasure in the fact that something awful…injury?…illness?…had rendered him all-but powerless like this?

Just the thought that she might be so…so *petty* made her feel ashamed of herself and as she picked up the tray laden with two steaming bowls of soup and a plate of crusty rolls she deliberately pinned a smile on her face.

'Lunch is served,' she said, then pulled a face. 'Although whether you can call it lunch at this time…'

'Actually…' Gregor halted uncomfortably and she noticed with escalating concern that his cheeks looked warmer than before.

Just how ill was he? Was his heightened colour just the result of the tablets taking away his pain or was his temperature rising?

'What's the matter?' She tried to be as dispassionately concerned as if he were just another of her patients, but this was Gregor, and she could never be dispassionate about him. 'Are you feeling worse? Do you need more tablets or—?'

'Nothing like that,' he dismissed quickly, but if anything his cheeks grew darker. 'It's just…well…before I put any more liquid into the system, I need to empty some out, so…'

Olivia almost laughed with relief that the problem was nothing more serious than that.

'That's no trouble,' she said airily with a glance towards the bathroom, glad, now that they hadn't had the money to do anything more than polish the existing wide-plank floorboards throughout the flat when they'd first bought it. Carpets would have made everything so much more difficult. 'Will you be able to manage, or…?' Remembering his insistence on getting himself in and out of the limousine made her hesitate to offer help.

'I don't even know whether I'll be able to get the chair in the room, let alone transfer myself onto—' He stopped abruptly when she chuckled, his expression darkening and those mobile lips flattening into a tight white line.

'Before you get on your high horse, thinking I'm mocking you, follow me and you'll see why I'm laughing,' she said, and set off across the room.

There were several silent seconds before she heard the muted squeak of the rubber tyres on the polished wood that told her he *was* following.

'Ta-da!' she said as she opened the bathroom door with a flourish to reveal the bright spacious room equipped with gleaming white chinaware.

The two of them had been planning the renovation of this room two years ago, just before he'd left for that last deployment, and she'd never thought she'd have the chance to show him how well it had turned out.

'You had it done!' he exclaimed with a gleam of pleasure in his eyes. 'It must have cost you a fortune to get it looking this good.'

'Actually, I did quite a bit of it myself,' she admitted, remembering how good it had felt to wield the sledgehammer while she'd demolished the wall that had separated the toilet into its own narrow little room. Sometimes it had seemed as if the sort of sheer hard physical labour that this project had involved had been the only way she'd been able to cope with the devastation of knowing that she would never see Gregor again, to say nothing of the fact that it had exhausted her enough to let her sleep without resorting to drugs. 'What do you think?'

He rolled himself into the room and as he swivelled to take in everything that had changed since he'd last been there, she saw the moment when he caught sight of the walk-in shower.

He laughed up at her with a new gleam in his eyes. 'You swore you'd be able to fit that in if it was the last thing you did!' he exclaimed with a flash of his old self that made her ache for all the time they'd lost; time that they could never regain.

'Well, you must admit that old shower dangling over the bath never did work very well, and this way I get to have my long lazy bath in peace—'

She stopped abruptly, silently cursing her tongue for running away with her when she remembered the way that argument had ended; hoping that, in the last two years, Gregor would have forgotten.

His raised a dark eyebrow and the pointed

glance at the shower that was definitely big enough for two to share told her that she wasn't that lucky.

'So…about the toilet…' She was definitely flustered by the graphic pictures inside her head; the ones in which she was sharing the top-of-the-line enclosure with Gregor and showering together wasn't what they were concentrating on.

'Yes. The toilet,' he echoed, but the expression on his face told her that he didn't need to be able to read her mind to know exactly what she'd been imagining because his thoughts had travelled the same steamy route.

It was several long seconds before he finally turned to examine the equipment in question and she was so rattled by the emotions he'd stirred inside her that she launched into speech.

'At least you can get to it now, but you probably won't be able to use it unaided without grab bars of some sort, so if you tell me what you want me to do so you can—'

'No!' he snapped, leaving her speechless as she took in the expression that darkened his face. 'I *don't* need help.'

'But you—'

'This is just temporary,' he interrupted fiercely, and she realised just how badly she'd stepped on his toes by automatically assuming he would need her help. It would have been far more productive—and far kinder on his intense independence—if she'd asked him whether he wanted her help.

'How temporary?' Perhaps she could use the opening he'd provided to get some of the answers she wanted.

'I've recently been through hours of orthopaedic and neurological testing and you know as well as I do that they have to take everything to the limit.'

'So, you're suffering from the next-day backlash with pain and loss of mobility?' He hadn't told her as much as she wanted to know, but at least the door had opened a tiny crack with the knowledge that those two departments had been involved.

'Exactly,' he said with barely a flicker, but she'd seen the way his eyes had momentarily dropped down and to the left, so she knew that he wasn't being entirely truthful. She was still going to have to do some probing before he gave her the whole story.

'So,' he continued, his attempt at appearing totally in control of the situation marred, somewhat, by the strain that seemed to draw the skin too tightly over his face, 'although I might curse and groan about it, I can manage perfectly well by myself if I put one hand on the side of the basin and the other on the radiator.'

She knew it was pointless to try to persuade him to accept her help, even if she stressed that it was only until the after-effects of all that testing had gone, but there was something she really needed to know and the only way to find out was to ask. 'Are your legs weight-bearing at all?'

Olivia heard the sharp hiss of indrawn breath, but it was swiftly silenced as his face settled into an expressionless mask.

'At the moment, not that you'd notice,' he admitted gruffly, then that stubborn chin stuck out obstinately. 'But I've been working on my upper-body strength, so there aren't many things I can't manage, one way or another.'

'In that case, I'll leave you to it…on the understanding that you won't be stupid about it. If you *do* need a hand, all you need to do is call me,' she said briskly, determined that she wouldn't reveal even a hint of how much his weakness terrified her, his stark admission about the lack of strength in his legs bringing home to her that she still had absolutely no idea what was wrong with him.

He silently held up a hand as she turned to leave the room and shrugged out of his jacket and for the first time she was able to get a closer look at some of the more delightful changes that had happened to his body since she'd last seen it.

He'd always had an impressive physical presence, with broad shoulders narrowing into lean, tight buttocks and long powerful legs, but the sheer muscle bulk that his current situation demanded was almost intimidating without the camouflage of a jacket.

'Livvy? Please…?' There was the same sort of rough edge to those two words that there would have been if she'd ogled him like that two years ago, but she couldn't imagine that was the same situation now, not when they were in the bathroom and he was waiting for her to leave.

Olivia couldn't meet his eyes as she hurried out

of the room, hoping that the warmth in her cheeks wasn't manifesting itself in a blush. For heaven's sake, she was a doctor! She discussed her patient's bodily functions all day, every day, so why was she getting all bent out of shape about them with her husband, of all people?

She definitely needed something else to concentrate on, and was wondering how easy it would be to get hold of the sort of grab bars Gregor would need to make his life easier. Then she was forced to remind herself that she had absolutely no idea if he was even going to be in the flat long enough to use the bathroom again, let alone staying for long enough to warrant the installation of the sort of aids that would ensure the degree of independence that would be essential to his peace of mind.

And that just brought her back full circle.

She'd had some time, now, to be hurt by the idea that he'd cared so little for her feelings that he'd allowed her to believe that he was dead, but the more she thought about the whole situation, at least there was one good thing to come out of it.

In a blinding flash of self-knowledge she realised that for the last two years she hadn't really come to terms with the enormity of every-thing she'd lost.

Oh, she'd put up a good front, throwing herself heart and soul into her career, but that had just been a way of trying to fill the gaping hole inside her where her love for Gregor and all the plans they'd made for their future had lived.

She could see, now, that she had virtually put her life on hold, switching off all her emotions because she just couldn't deal with the pain of so great a loss.

And for what?

'Livvy?'

Somehow, the unexpected hint of uncertainty in Gregor's voice behind her, signalling his silent return to the living room, brought all the ingre-dients inside her to a rolling boil that only grew hotter when she whirled to face him and saw him sitting there, still essentially the same man she'd loved and married and yet, obviously, so very different.

'Why did you do it, Gregor?' she demanded hotly, her hands clenched tightly into fists, her nails digging into her palms as she fought the urge to scream at him instead.

'Do what?' He had the gall to look puzzled and that only stoked her anger.

'Why did you stay away like that…without a word? Why did you let them…the army…lie to me…let me believe you were dead? If you didn't love me any more…didn't want to be married any more…wouldn't it have been kinder…more straightforward…just to tell me…to ask for a divorce, or…or…?'

It was only when she realised that she couldn't see him properly any more and that she couldn't draw in enough breath to utter another word that it dawned on her that, after two long years of holding all the agony in, the floodgates were finally about to burst.

CHAPTER THREE

No! No tears yet!

And not in front of Gregor, she told herself fiercely, tightening her fists and blinking hard as she concentrated on the sharp pain as each nail dug into her palm to keep the tears at bay.

For several interminable seconds they stared at each other, Gregor sitting so still and silent that she wondered if he was even breathing.

'Gregor—'

'Not yet, Livvy,' he growled, and it was only then that she realised just how exhausted he was under that thin veneer of invincibility.

And how much of that was due to pain? she wondered.

And how much worse was that pain because he refused to allow her to help him?

Her heart clenched inside, because, no matter

how angry she was at the way he'd treated her,
this was the man she'd loved more than any other
in the world…the man she was afraid she would
always love, no matter what might happen to
their relationship.

'Has the analgesia started working yet?' she
asked stiffly, taking refuge in the medical background that had initially brought them together.
Perhaps if she treated him with the same professional distance as a patient it would make the
whole situation easier.

'Not yet,' he admitted. 'It seems to take at least
twenty minutes before it starts to be effective.'

'How long have you been on it? Long enough
for your body to become accustomed to it…to
need the dose increased?' She shuddered at the
thought that whatever was wrong with him
might need even stronger painkillers than the
ones he was taking. He'd blamed his current
condition on the contortions he'd been put
through at the hospital, but if there was some
serious underlying problem…one that was only
going to worsen with time…

'I've only been on these for the last couple of
days, and if it hadn't been for the taxi journey and

hauling myself in and out of the car, I'd been hoping I might be able to start easing off on them, but then I forgot to take a dose today and…' He shrugged rather than complete the sentence and when she found her attention drawn inexorably to the powerful swells of muscle outlined to perfection by the light shining through the thin cotton of his shirt, she had to drag herself away before she made a complete fool of herself.

Suddenly needing the activity to keep her hands busy and her eyes away from him, she hurried across to transfer the bowls of soup to the microwave long enough to heat them up again.

How crazy was it that, even when she was so angry with him…so hurt by the cavalier way he'd abandoned her…all she wanted to do was reach out to touch him…needing to put her hands on his shoulders…to feel their width and test their reassuringly solid power, to cradle the familiar shape of his head between her palms and trace each one of his features to confirm what her eyes were telling her—that her beloved Gregor really was alive in front of her.

'Here. The warm liquid might help to speed the absorption of the drugs into your system,' she said prosaically, torn between her unquenchable urge to take care of him and her need for answers.

It took a moment before he brought the first spoonful to his mouth and Olivia wondered if he was feeling the same clenched ache of stress in his belly that was robbing her of any appetite. Then the taste must have hit his tastebuds because, with a soft murmur of pleasure, he took a larger second mouthful and then a third.

'You always did make fantastic soups,' he murmured as he reached for one of the home-made rolls and broke off a mouthful. 'And I'd forgotten how good these are…how much better than bought bread.'

The unexpected compliments spread a warm glow through her and suddenly she discovered that her own appetite had returned, too.

It was only when they both sat back with their bowls scraped clean that the tension returned, and this time Olivia didn't bother to try to dispel it by starting to clear the table.

'No more evasion, Gregor. No more delaying tactics,' she said seriously, even though her heart felt as if it was trying to beat its way out through her throat. 'I deserve some straight answers, so, where have you been for the last two years?'

'In hell,' he said, so fiercely that she blinked.

She nearly scoffed at the facile answer, but then she caught a glimpse of the shadows in his eyes and paused a moment to take a closer look.

A swift cataloguing of his white-knuckled fists and the tension in his face told her that he was telling her nothing less than he believed to be true, and knowing that he wasn't a man given to exaggeration, she could well believe it, too.

'Where was this hell…or would you have to kill me if you told me?' she added, resurrecting the joke that had been batted backwards and forwards between them ever since he'd explained about his years of commitment to the army in return for their sponsorship through medical school.

'How much were you told?' he asked, and she was struck by the same urge to scream that hit her every time he got that wary look. But where was the sense in trying to take her frustration out on him? If he wasn't allowed to tell her where he'd been, she was just going to have to accept that there was a good reason for it.

'Not much,' she said tightly. 'Just that you were in the wrong place at the wrong time when there was an explosion, and that, because of the situation at the time, they'd been unable to retrieve your body to bring it back for burial.'

Her throat ached with the memory that she hadn't even been able to have a proper funeral for him; that there had been nothing and nowhere for her to focus her loss…other than a formal memorial service attended by a succession of smartly-uniformed well-wishers with chests full of medals. 'They didn't tell me anything more than that. Apparently, they never *do* tell you any more than they absolutely have to, even though it should be the family's right to know how and where they lost their loved one.'

'It isn't always possible,' he pointed out, far too calmly for her liking. 'Telling families the details might make things easier for those left behind, but if it compromises the safety of those still in the field…of your colleagues…'

'But you weren't supposed to be "in the field", for heaven's sake!' she exclaimed hotly. 'You're a qualified doctor, and your posting was to a field hospital where you'd be in charge of patching-up the injured so they could be shipped out to a proper hospital.'

Again, she felt the scalding press of frustrated tears that had been dammed up too long, and had to draw in a deep breath and bite her lips together to prevent the tell-tale drops from starting.

What had made the whole situation so much worse to bear was that it was supposed to have been his final deployment before he would be free to leave the army, his service commitment finally completed. She'd been so looking forward to the two of them being able to start their married life properly at last, to be able to choose where they went, and when, for the first time on holiday since they'd met. They'd even begun, tentatively, to talk about starting a family…

'In conflict situations, circumstances can change very quickly,' he explained patiently, not for the first time, dragging her away from pointless painful re-runs of what might have been. 'Sometimes the place where it was thought safe to set up the casualty unit can, in a very few hours, suddenly be right in the middle of the front line.'

She could tell he was choosing his words with care, but even so, the mental images of Gregor stabilising post-operative patients in safety one minute only to have shells exploding all around him the next was one that had given her nightmares ever since she'd realised just what his job entailed.

Each time he went off for a new posting she'd had to resign herself to night after night of broken sleep until he returned to her in one piece, but the nightmares had only become unbearable when she'd been told he'd died, so that even exhaustion hadn't been able to guarantee her a good night's sleep.

'So, is that what happened to you—to your back?' she asked, suddenly almost hopeful that a traumatic injury was the reason why he was confined to the wheelchair rather than a fatal illness. 'Does it all date from the accident two years ago?'

'Apparently,' he said with a grimace. 'I'm afraid I don't remember.'

'You don't remember…*what*, exactly? The circumstances that put you in the wrong place at the wrong time? Or the accident itself?' She knew that traumatic amnesia was relatively common; that many people never remembered the events leading up to life-threatening accidents, even if the memory loss was only of the few seconds surrounding the impact.

'None of it,' he admitted grimly, staring blankly out towards the park where the fading day was wreathing mist around the trees. 'The first memory I have is very hazy…so hazy that I'm not even sure that it *is* a memory. Perhaps I'm picturing it because I've been told about it…' His forehead pleated in concentration, his unfairly long eyelashes casting shadows over the sharp angles and flat planes of cheekbones that were far more prominent than the last time she'd seen him. Was that because he'd lost so much weight or because his injuries caused him so much pain?

'There was a child…' he said haltingly, 'several children…young children, but especially one…a little girl with big dark eyes and curly hair.' His own dark eyes were wide but obviously focused only on the images he was seeing inside his head. 'She was patting my face, very gently, and telling me it was time to wake up.'

'And then?' Olivia hardly dared to speak, afraid that the interruption would make him realise he was telling her more than he should.

'The next thing I remember is being surrounded by men in heavy muddy boots, all of them shouting at each other over the top of me and waving guns around.' He gave a wintry smile. 'Apparently, I tugged on the trouser-leg of one of them and told him they were making my head ache.'

That startled a chuckle out of her. The fact that he was sometimes sent to some of the most dangerous places on the globe had always terrified her, but there had always been something that was just so…so *competent* about him that she could easily picture him surrounded by the toughest of the tough and asking them to keep the noise down.

Whatever else she might criticise about him, he'd never been short of courage, which made his absence from her life all the more incomprehensible, given the fact that he hadn't died after all. So surely, if he hadn't wanted to be married to her any more, he would have found some straightforward way to tell her. Wouldn't he?

Before she could frame that thought into a question, she was interrupted by the strident martial tones of 'The Ride of the Valkyrie' on her mobile phone.

'Ignore it,' Gregor urged as she reached for it, but the action was automatic after so many years on call; she could no more ignore a ringing phone than she could take off and fly around the room.

Besides, she didn't need to look at the number on the caller display to know who was calling, not after assigning such an appropriate ring tone to the person trying to reach her.

'It's my mother,' she muttered, hesitating. She really didn't want to answer because she could already guess the content of the conversation— it was all too predictable, unlike the far more important one she'd been having with Gregor.

'I suppose you'll have to answer it, then. She'll only keep ringing until you do,' he said in a resigned tone, then manoeuvred his chair away from the table as though to give her some semblance of privacy.

'Olivia!' He might as well have saved himself the trouble, she thought as her mother's cut-glass accent resounded through the flat, her abiding distrust of the latest technology apparently making her believe that the smaller the phone, the louder she had to shout to be heard.

'Yes, Mother,' she said, then held the phone at arm's length for the sake of her eardrums.

'Where are you?' her mother demanded. 'Parker came back with some nonsense about dropping you off at the airport.'

For just a second her eyes met Gregor's and they shared a guilty grin, but she had no idea that she was going to perpetuate the myth until she actually heard the words emerging from her own mouth.

'You only just rang me in time,' she said, her brain rapidly juggling phrases that would get the message across without telling a deliberate lie. 'All phones have to be turned off before take-off. Apparently, it's so that they don't make the fuel tanks explode or interfere with the electronic guidance systems or something. I'll call you when I get the chance.'

Well, airlines *did* insist that all electronic gadgetry was switched off, and if she and Gregor *had* been on board a flight about to take off…

'Olivia! Don't you *dare* turn this phone off!

There are things we need to discuss, meetings we need to organise with the solicitors before you—'

Olivia pressed the button to end the call then immediately turned the phone completely off and, in spite of a shiver of guilt, suddenly felt as if someone had just lifted an enormous weight off her shoulders.

'Any bets on how many messages she'll leave before you switch it back on?' Gregor asked wryly.

'Probably more than eleven,' she retorted, and they shared another fleeting grin at the shared memory of the exact number of messages they'd come back to after their twenty-four-hour honeymoon. The final message had actually threatened Gregor with a nationwide manhunt for kidnap if he didn't return Olivia to her family immediately.

'Even though we were both well over the age of consent,' he murmured, demonstrating that he hadn't lost the knack of being able to follow her train of thought.

As if that would ever make a difference to her mother, Olivia mused. She could imagine the woman still thinking that she had the right to order her daughter about and organise her life for the next thirty years, at least. The small matter that Olivia had held down a highly qualified responsible career for several years and even the undisputable fact of a marriage hadn't stopped her, so far.

'Do you think she'll ever give up trying to marry you off to someone *suitable*?' he asked wryly. 'She must have thought she'd cracked it this time, with the Grayson-Smythes. Imagine… the two family estates finally joined together and the next generation of the Mannington-Forbes bloodline with a hereditary title!'

That had never been on the cards, Olivia thought, everything inside her repulsed by the very idea of carrying any but Gregor's child. In fact, it was unlikely, now, that she'd ever have a child of her own if Gregor did want a divorce.

And if that wasn't a thought to make her heart sink and add an extra few decibels to the thumping going on inside her head, she turned round and saw that, in spite of the heavy-duty medication, Gregor was looking positively grey again.

'What time have you got to be back at the hospital?' she asked, knowing that neither of them was really in the right frame of mind to sort anything out tonight. Anyway, with the wedding called off, there really wasn't any rush to sort the divorce out, was there? The pang of disappointment that their time together had been so brief was something she couldn't afford to think about.

'I don't,' he said firmly.

She frowned. The label on his analgesics had been dispensed by the pharmacy in her own hospital and she'd already registered the fact that it would normally only be administered to an in-patient.

'You mean, you haven't got a curfew? Surely they want you back before the ward settles down for the night, otherwise you'll disturb everyone else.'

'I don't have to go back because I signed myself out—AMA,' he said, his tone almost belligerent.

'But...' He'd left the hospital against medical advice? Well, it didn't take her medical qualifications to see that he still needed...

'I couldn't stand it any longer,' he added grimly, swivelling the chair to face her. 'Livvy, today was almost the first time in nearly two years that I've been outside some sort of medical institution. I've had enough of doctors to last me a lifetime, but…I just needed…'

He didn't need to finish the thought. The edge of despair in his voice was matched by the shadows in his eyes and the tension stiffening his whole body.

The part of her that would always love this man ached to know everything that had happened to him since the last time she'd seen him, but now was not the right time…not when his medical condition seemed to have been aggravated by all the tests he'd been through.

'So, what have you planned to do?' she asked. 'I wouldn't have thought they'd be happy to have you discharge yourself when you're on such high doses of analgesia; but then, I suppose you told them you weren't in much pain.'

'There wasn't time for much of a discussion about it,' he admitted. 'I was just glancing through one of those glossy magazines and caught sight of your photo with…' He paused for her to supply the name of the man who'd accompanied her in the stylised shot.

'Ash…Ashley Grayson-Smythe,' she supplied with an inner wince, knowing exactly which photo he meant and blaming her mother anew for contacting the publication with the announcement of the impending wedding. That had been the single incident that had set the awful roller-coaster on its apparently unstoppable journey.

'It was an out-of-date issue, the way they usually are in hospitals and doctors' surgeries,' he continued, 'and when I realised that the wedding was due to happen today, all I was focused on was getting there in time to prevent you making the dreadful social *faux pas* of committing bigamy.'

'Well, I'm sure that once the Grayson-Smythe and the Mannington-Forbes families have had time to recover from today's debacle, they'll be properly grateful for your efforts,' she said crisply, 'but that still doesn't tell me where you were intending to go after you'd disrupted all my mother's careful planning.'

'I hadn't arranged anything,' he admitted, with a sideways glance in her direction that gave her just a glimpse of those unforgettable silver eyes.

But, then, a glimpse had always been enough to send a shiver of awareness through her and distract her from whatever she was doing. 'I was hoping…well…that you would let me stay here.'

'*Here?*'

That was the last thing she'd been expecting…although if she were to be honest, something deep inside her clenched tight with excitement just at the thought of having Gregor home again.

Home?

If that wasn't the craziest thought she'd had today.

The flat they'd chosen together and lived in right up until he'd disappeared out of her life hadn't been Gregor's home for nearly two years. Where did he get off expecting to swan back in? Next, he'd be asking her to take care of him until…until whatever was wrong with him had resolved itself, one way or another?

Or, until their divorce papers came through?

In spite of the fact that she knew he was probably the most stubbornly independent man on the planet, indignation roared through her, mixed with disbelief that he could just blithely assume that he had the right to move back in when he hadn't bothered to let her know—

'Please?' he added softly, his voice rough around the edges with the sort of bone-deep exhaustion she'd never heard from him before, and even though she'd been drawing breath to blast him with a few home truths, she knew the battle was lost.

'For how long?' she demanded, trying to fight a rearguard action even though she knew it was pointless. She never had been able to refuse him anything, almost from the first moment she'd met him, especially when there was a hint of that pleading-little-boy look on his face. There was just something so—

'I'll have to make another appointment at the hospital to replace the one I missed this morning, and then...' Something dark flashed across his face but it was so quickly hidden that she could have been mistaken, especially when he added in an upbeat voice, 'If I could just stay here until I'm on my feet?'

The almost casual reference to his present disability and the implication that his condition wasn't expected to be permanent made her quite giddy with relief.

'And how long is that likely to be?' Was her delight at the news hidden behind her attempt at a poker face? It was becoming harder and harder to remember just why she should be angry with him; why she should resent his easy impression that he could just slip back into her life as easily as he'd left it.

'Does it make a difference?' he asked after a telling pause. 'Livvy, I don't exactly have too many options at the moment. With the change in the law, public accessibility is apparently improving for those less physically able, but I'm not in a fit state to deal with the attention I'd draw if I booked into a hotel, nor am I mobile enough to book into the nearest motel. And you have to admit that there's no chance of going flat-hunting and expecting to find something I could move into tonight…'

The utter weariness that accompanied his observations surrounded him like a suffocating fog and made her feel like a poisonous witch, especially when the long fraught day was almost drawing to a close.

This was the man she'd promised to love and

honour in sickness and in health, and just because he'd disappeared for two years, it didn't absolve her from keeping those promises, not while they were still legally married...and even if they *weren't* still married, she probably wouldn't be able to forget those promises for a good deal longer than that, if she was honest.

'You'd better take the bedroom,' she conceded. 'There's room to manoeuvre the chair in there and you'll have easier access to the bathroom.'

She started to clear the table and when, out of the corner of her eye, she saw him clench his hands around the arms of his chair, she knew that he was regretting the fact that he wasn't able to help her with even that menial task; something he'd never shied from during their marriage.

'If you go on through, you can take your time getting ready. I'll finish tidying up in here, but I'll be listening in case you need to shout for help,' she suggested, hoping to give both of them a few moments of breathing space before she had to face the reality of having Gregor back in her life and in their bed again. And in spite of the fact he'd been gone for two years, it was going to be hard to come to terms with the fact that it felt so right to have him back.

'I can manage alone,' he said brusquely, and even though Olivia knew that there was no point in showing her frustration as male pride took precedence over common sense, it was still difficult not to let her anger show when she whirled to confront him.

'So your tendency towards being pig-headed hasn't diminished over the last couple of years,' she snapped, and continued before he had the chance to do more than draw a defensive breath, 'Just tell me, how much damage is your stubbornness likely to do to you? You haven't even told me what's the matter with you…why you need the chair.'

Suddenly, something he'd said a few minutes ago came roaring back into her head.

Today was the first time in nearly two years that he'd been out of a medical institution? Where on earth had he been? And if he'd been injured in the line of duty, as she'd been told two years ago, surely the army should have been responsible for looking after him. In which case, why hadn't she been informed when he'd been found?

'I've had several bouts of surgery to put various bits back together,' he said tersely. 'I now have enough pins and plates and screws in me to set off a major alert if I go to an airport.'

'Was the surgery successful?' She wondered briefly what the chances were that she'd be able to have a look at his medical notes. The likelihood that Gregor would give her the full details of what he'd gone through was slim to none if the previous time he'd come home after working forty-eight hours straight through with half a dozen broken ribs was anything to go by.

'Which surgery?' He pulled a wry face. 'Probably none of it was as successful as if it had been done properly, two years ago,' he muttered with a grimace. 'But at least there's a chance that I'll—'

'What do you mean, not as successful as if it had been done two years ago?' she interrupted. 'You mean, all your operations were necessary to correct injuries that happened nearly two years ago? Not for something that happened recently?' The idea that the treatment he needed had been withheld from him utterly horrified her.

'The sort of surgery I needed wasn't... wasn't available,' he said grimly, and she knew from the way he'd worded his answer and from the tone of his voice that she wouldn't be getting any further details from him...at least, not until he was ready to give them to her.

She stifled a sigh, knowing that brow-beating would never work with this stubborn man, yet aching with the need to do something... anything...to make things easier for him.

Except...did she have the right any more? Two years was a long time for a man as virile and attractive as Gregor. Perhaps there was someone else in his life, now; someone whose help he *would* welcome.

'Go through to the bedroom. And remember to shout if you need a hand,' she suggested, knowing that call was unlikely to come.

Even with her back to him she knew exactly when he left the room. There was a strange electricity that had always sparked when they were near each other and it didn't seem to have lessened in the time they'd been apart.

She smiled sadly as she remembered the first time he'd come back to her from his very first front-line deployment.

For weeks her nerves had been strung tighter than violin strings, refusing to believe anything but that he would return home safely to her. And then, without a word of warning, the door had opened and he'd been there, sunburnt and windblown and with the wild fire of over-whelming desire in his eyes that hadn't subsided to a manageable simmer until they'd finally emerged from the bedroom more than twenty-four hours later.

How different things were now, she thought sadly, swallowing the tight ache in her throat as she wasted time fluffing cushions and straight-ening books around the living room even as she strained to hear what Gregor was doing.

The flat was as neat as a show-home when she heard the first mutterings and she was torn between the urge to laugh and the need to cry when she recognised it for what it was.

Gregor may have left his own country in his early teens and his English was almost perfect, but in moments of stress he still reverted to pro-fanities in his own tongue.

'I can swear without shocking anyone,' he'd said the first time she'd heard him letting off steam. Although with the recent addition of a number of East European countries into the jobs market, he might have to learn to be a little more circumspect from now on…

On silent stockinged feet she made her way to the bedroom door to lean against the frame, folding her arms while she took in the situation that was causing Gregor's bad temper.

For a moment shock robbed her of the power to breathe when she saw him there, sitting in the chair in nothing more than his underwear.

What on earth had he been through to do this to his body?

He'd been the perfect specimen of manhood in its prime the last time she'd seen him in this room, his broad shoulders tapering into a lean waist and his arms and legs beautifully muscled under smooth bronzed skin dusted with dark whorls of silky hair.

This man was so utterly different that she could almost have walked past him without recognising him if he'd been a patient on the ward.

His shoulders were broader than ever, with extra bulk to the powerful layer of muscles as a result of having to haul himself in and out of the chair. His torso had always been lean and taut but that six-pack was so perfectly sculpted now that her fingers itched to trace the symmetry of those ridges. But where were those muscular thighs that had been strong enough to power him out of a chair even with her weight in his arms, and the calf muscles that had reminded her of Michelangelo's David? Never had she expected Gregor's legs to look so pale and wasted…more like an elderly man than one in the prime of life.

And where was the healthy glow on the natural bronze of his skin that had tempted her to touch…to explore all that silky warmth and furrow through the swirls of dark hair? The grey cast to his body, now, made it all-too evident just how long it had been since he'd last been well.

'Problem?' she asked mildly, unable to leave him struggling when there was the chance that he might do himself damage. 'Were you just about to call for me?'

She saw the muscles in his jaw tense rhythmically as he fought down his ire. 'The bed is too soft to brace myself to transfer out of the chair,' he said stiffly.

'Would you be able to manage better if I were to put a board under the mattress? I could get one tomorrow,' she suggested as she stepped forward, hoping she sounded calmer than she felt, especially as she'd just implied that he'd be staying for more than one night. 'What position do you prefer…?' She swallowed down the rest of the sentence, suddenly realising just how it sounded, but the damage was already done.

'Livvy…' Gregor growled, his eyes every bit as dark and hot as they'd been in her memories, and her heart stuttered wildly for several breathless seconds.

Every fibre of her being longed for the last two years to disappear; for everything to be exactly as it had been when he'd swept her into his arms just moments before he'd been due to depart for that final deployment, unable to resist making love for one last time.

Then she saw him blink, deliberately, and it was almost as if a screen had come down, shutting her out from any evidence of what he was thinking and feeling.

Her heart clenched inside her with this fresh evidence that what had once been between them had been damaged for ever in the two years they'd been apart, but that wouldn't stop her doing what was necessary to take care of him.

'Link your hands behind my neck,' she directed after a moment's thought, positioning herself squarely in front of him.

Silently, he complied, although every inch of him screamed resentment that he needed her assistance.

It was a mixture of heaven and hell to wrap her arms around him and pull him tight against her body and she had to concentrate on the simple mechanics of lifting him just enough to clear the chair before she could pivot him so that she could lower him onto the bed.

She bent to take the weight of his lower legs, not giving him time to object to the assistance before she lifted them onto the bed, but it was only when Gregor turned away from her to grab the edge of the covers to pull them over himself that she had her first sight of the livid scars marring his lower back.

It was only the briefest heart-stopping glimpse but it was all the evidence she needed to realise just how close he'd come to losing his life entirely.

Some were jagged—ugly reminders of the injuries inflicted on him by the explosion—while others were neatly outlined by the punctuation of stitches that proved that some sort of attempt had been made to piece him back together in the intervening years.

'Oh, Gregor,' she breathed, her heart aching for him and everything he'd lost in the blink of an eye, but the expression on his face as he settled himself against the pillows told her any sympathy she tried to show would only be taken as pity.

It seemed wrong that her breasts were still tingling from the taut pressure of those beautifully developed pectorals and she wasn't expecting to be distracted by the sight of his dark head against the pale blue pillow she usually slept on, but the last thing she anticipated was that he would grab her hand before she could walk away.

'Is there something else you need me to do?' she asked, overwhelmingly aware of the leashed strength in his grip and the fact that she could now smell the scent of her own soap on his skin and her toothpaste on his breath.

For several endless seconds she caught a

glimpse of the turmoil that raged inside him but then he released her with almost insulting haste.

'I don't think so, Livvy,' he said, rawly. 'You've tucked me in, but I think we'd better forgo the kiss goodnight, under the circumstances, don't you?'

CHAPTER FOUR

OLIVIA had no idea what woke her.

She'd made herself a bed on the make-shift single tucked against one wall in the room that was now her office, then, in spite of her exhausting day, had found that her brain refused to switch off.

She hadn't even realised that she'd fallen asleep, having lain there for ages in the dark imagining she could hear Gregor breathing at the other end of the flat.

She could certainly hear something now.

'*Janek? Oksana!*' came a hoarse shout.

That was definitely Gregor's voice, and before she even realised she was moving, she was out of the door and speeding towards his room.

'Gregor?' She didn't know what reflex had her pulling her hand away from the light before she had a chance to turn it on. Probably the memories of the misery she'd suffered in boarding school when the bedroom lights had been unceremoniously switched on as the bells had rung each morning.

Anyway, the bar of light from the open door was streaming far enough across the bed to tell her that Gregor definitely hadn't been calling out for *her*.

In fact, from the agitated way his head was tossing and turning against the pillow, it was unlikely that he was awake at all.

His sudden groan made her jump, especially when it was followed by an indecipherable shout and what was obviously a stream of invective.

Olivia's eyes stung with the threat of helpless tears while she hovered by the side of the bed, uncertain what to do for the best.

He'd had nightmares before when he'd come back from some of his deployments, and when she'd tried to ask him about them had airily passed them off as one of the inconveniences of the job. But this was something more than that; something far worse.

And what about his back? How much harm

could he be doing to himself? He'd been in so much pain today, doing nothing more than sitting in his wheelchair. How much damage could he be doing twisting and turning like that?

'Gregor?' she called again, and warily reached out a soothing hand towards his naked shoulder.

She only just remembered in time the moment, in the early days of their relationship, when she'd playfully grabbed him when he'd only been half-awake. In an instant, she'd found herself pinned to the floor with his forearm across her throat and a murderous expression in his eyes.

'Gregor…Gregor Davidov!' she called, sharpening her tone and making her voice as close to authoritarian as she could when she was trembling all over. She had absolutely no idea what instinct had her using the original form of his surname rather than the Anglicised one he'd been using ever since he'd come to England.

To her relief he grew still…almost eerily still when his breathing was too fast and his pulse was racing in the hollow at the base of his throat.

'Gregor, are you awake?' she demanded in a softer tone. 'Do you know where you are?'

She was almost holding her breath while she

waited to see if he would answer and was quite light-headed with relief when his husky voice sounded in the gloom.

'Yes, Livvy. I know where I am,' he said with a sigh. 'I'm sorry. Obviously, I woke you. Was I making so much noise?'

'Not so much,' she temporised. 'I was just worried that you were in pain and I remembered that I'd left your tablets out on the dining table. Do you want me to get them for you?'

He was silent and she shivered with the sudden awareness that she was standing just inches away from his largely naked body wearing nothing more than an over-sized T-shirt. She only hoped the light wasn't good enough for him to see that her cheeks sported a fiery blush, or that he could recognise that it was one of *his* T-shirts that she'd taken to wearing for emotional comfort when she'd believed she'd never see him again.

It was only by the slightest glitter of reflected light that she could tell that he was looking at her, and just when the silence had stretched to the point of embarrassment he spoke, gruffly. 'Please. Then I'll need to go to the bathroom, too,' and she realised that she'd also left his chair too far away for him to reach unaided.

They would get beyond this, she reminded herself while she hovered outside the bathroom just in case Gregor called her for help. She would learn to put things where he needed them to be so that he could be as independent as possible, and hopefully there was the prospect that he wouldn't be needing that level of help for very long. Otherwise, she didn't know whether she would be able to hang on to her sanity; not when she was having to work so hard to seem unmoved by his plight; not when she knew he would hate to be pitied; not when her stupid heart just wanted to wrap him safely in her arms and refuse to let him out of her sight ever again.

Unfortunately, the sooner he didn't need her any more, the sooner he could be insisting that the legalities for ending their marriage were put in motion, but in spite of her anger that he'd left her for two years thinking he was dead, she recognised that it would be selfish in the extreme to hope that his recovery took any longer than necessary.

Olivia recognised that Gregor's groan as he subsided onto the bed again was one of mixed frustration and exhaustion, and she wasn't surprised when he fell asleep almost immediately, no doubt helped by the recent dose of analgesia.

She wasn't surprised, either, when she found herself hesitating in the doorway, unable to make herself walk away from him when he was lying there, in their bed, for the first night in two long years.

It only took a moment to unfold the antique quilt draped over the end of the bed to wrap it around her shoulders, and once she was settled in the wing chair she'd lovingly restored in the long lonely evenings during one of Gregor's earlier deployments, there was nothing to stop her giving in to the sheer pleasure of looking at him lying there…the man she'd never stopped loving even at the height of her anger and the depths of her despair.

He'd always been a good-looking man, dark haired and with those amazing silvery eyes that seemed all the more unearthly surrounded by such long dark lashes. His face was a sculptor's delight, composed of the sort of lean planes and strong lines that would still look good no matter how old he was.

And that body…

One of her worst nightmares when she'd been told about the way he'd died had been the devastation her vivid imagination had painted of the effect of his injuries on the body she'd delighted in exploring.

She pressed her clenched fists into her belly in an attempt at quelling the visceral reaction she'd always had when she remembered the first time she'd seen him naked.

If ever a man could be said to have a beautiful body…that would be Gregor.

He must have been born with the perfect combination of genes to give him the classic broad shoulders, slim hips and long legs that had been seen as the epitome of male perfection ever since mankind had first started drawing on cave walls. In his case, even though he'd loathed the narcissistic body-building mentality of most men who frequented gyms, his dedication to being in the peak of fitness to fulfil his duty towards his colleagues meant that he'd always taken care of himself with a good diet and fitness regimen, and she'd thoroughly appreciated every lean muscular inch of the results.

It had been a real shock to see those once powerful legs looking so weak; to see him tremble with the effort of holding the weight of his body. Before, he'd thought nothing of carrying her in his arms all way up the stairs to the flat when his desire for her had been so urgent that he couldn't be bothered to wait for the ancient lift to arrive.

At least, in the shadowy darkness of the bedroom, his chest looked much the same. Against his pallid skin, the dark whorls of hair still formed an intriguing crucifix from one tight male nipple to the other and right down the centre of his body to disappear under the bedclothes at his waist.

Her fingertips tingled with the need to trace that pattern; to know if the dark hair still felt as silky as she remembered and if the strands would still coil themselves around her exploring fingers.

Suddenly, Gregor began to grow restless again, his dark tousled head tossing restlessly against the pillow and his chest rising and falling irregularly with his agitation.

'Gregor,' she called softly, hoping her tone

would sound soothing if it reached him through the dark images plaguing him. 'Gregor, you're dreaming again. It's only a dream.'

'*Janek*,' he moaned, his distress increasing, and she knew she had to do something, even at the risk of a few bruises of her own. She'd learned to her cost that startling him awake in the first few days after he returned from a deployment was likely to result in finding herself pinned down by a man who was every inch a warrior prepared to fight for his life.

'Gregor, it's me…it's Livvy. I'm here,' she said as she grabbed his nearest hand between both of hers and held on tightly. 'You're safe now, Gregor… I'm here.'

As if the physical contact between them was a signal, his eyes flicked open, the silvery irises only a slender gleam around the darkly dilated pupils as he stared wildly up at her.

'The children,' he gasped hoarsely. 'Save the children. Please…help me. I must save the children.'

Olivia felt her own eyes grow wide.

Children? What children? No one had mentioned children to her so she'd automatically assumed that he'd been with his colleagues when the explosion had happened…but, then, they'd told her as little as they could when they'd informed her that Gregor would never be coming home again.

And, anyway, this definitely wasn't the time to ask.

'You're safe, Gregor. It's all over,' she told him. 'The children are safe,' she added, mentally crossing her fingers that it was true. The thought that there might have been defenceless children in the area where he'd been so badly injured just didn't bear thinking about.

He stared up at her for a long time and she could almost hear the cogs whirring in his brain while he tried to sort out the facts from the images inside his head.

Her back started to complain about being hunched over the side of the bed—just one of the unpleasant penalties of working long hours in Accident and Emergency—and she gingerly perched one hip on the edge of the mattress to ease the strain.

'Livvy,' he said on a shuddering sigh, and she felt the tension begin to leak out of him like the start of the spring thaw after a long hard winter. 'Is it really you, at last?'

His other hand reached out tentatively to trace the side of her face with gentle fingertips, lingering at the corner of her mouth for several heart-stopping seconds.

'I dreamed about you,' he said softly, and she couldn't help chuckling.

'So that's why you're having nightmares?' she teased.

'Not you. Not nightmares.' The words were swift and fervent. 'Even when I didn't know who you were, I dreamed of you, and seeing your face made me feel...'

He stopped speaking suddenly, as though he'd said too much, but before her old frustration could surface, he continued in a voice she'd never heard before. 'For more than a year, my head was filled with terrible images...explosions...people... bodies...parts of bodies...flying through the air with dirt, rocks, pieces of buildings. And the noise...' Even in the muted light she could see him shake his head. 'It was like the worst vision of hell, and I was living in it.'

'You were re-living the explosion when you

were injured?' she suggested, for the first time since she'd begun her medical training feeling completely out of her depth. The brief time they'd spent learning about psychology and psychiatry certainly hadn't equipped her for anything more than to recognise when a patient needed to be referred to someone with greater expertise.

'That's what I thought, for a long time,' he said heavily. 'I presumed that it was a symptom of post-traumatic stress, in the time when I couldn't remember what I did for a living.'

'Even so, as an army medic, you're usually involved with patching people up well enough for them to be shipped off to the nearest hospital. You haven't been anywhere near the explosions before…as far as I know,' she added meaningfully, and caught a glimpse of his wry grimace acknowledging her point.

'And, of course, no-one knew who I was or who I was connected with in the region—there were at least two armies that were government controlled, ours and theirs, as well as various private outfits of thugs and mercenaries that were far better equipped through drug money—so there was no-one with the expertise to make a diagnosis or get me treatment to deal with any of it.'

There were so many issues buried in just that one rambling sentence that it would take hours to talk them through, but for the moment Olivia reasoned that it was just better to let him speak; to let him choose his own way through the thoughts and images that filled his head.

'It was only recently... There had been aid workers almost before it was safe for them to be there, but then there was a crew who arrived to begin some of the massive reconstruction that was needed in the area, and some of them were ex-forces...electrical and mechanical engineers, mainly, but a couple of them had some paramedic training...' He gave a brief, disbelieving laugh. 'You have no idea how weird it was to hear someone say, "Bloody 'ell, Doc, what're *you* doin' 'ere? You're supposed to be dead," in a broad Yorkshire accent.'

Olivia managed to chuckle, but it was a watery affair, almost drowned under her growing need to cry for everything he'd endured.

'Suddenly, it was as though someone had flicked a switch on inside my head and I remem-

bered that my name hadn't been Gregor Davidov
for a long time. Unfortunately, I also remembered what had been going on before I ended up
in the hospital,' he ended on a sombre note.

'How much can you tell me?' she prompted
softly, aching with the need to hold him; to
reassure him that she was there for him…
would always be there for him because, no
matter what else happened between them, she
would always love him.

'There were children…a whole school full of
children—some of them refugees from the
fighting, but most of them from the surrounding
villages—all ages from five years old to about
ten or eleven. It was close enough that they could
hear the fighting going on in the distance, but
everyone said they were safe and so were we and
our patients. Then, suddenly, there were shells
coming in our direction, closer and closer, and
we were told to pack up; to get everyone into
some sort of transport and grab as much of the
equipment as we could.'

He was silent for some time, but she didn't
push, guessing that he'd become lost in the
memories for a moment.

'We'd done it in record time and were just pulling out,' he resumed, a touch of gravel roughening his voice. 'The road ran quite near the school and someone ran towards the column of vehicles shouting and waving his arms. They nearly shot him, thinking he was some sort of decoy for an ambush,' he said, the words coming faster and faster. 'Then we realised he was asking for help, saying that the school had been damaged. The children were trapped in the cellar, where he'd taken them for safety, and there was an old boiler down there that could explode at any minute.'

'So, you went to help,' she said quietly, wondering how and when she'd ended up on the side of the bed with him, her arms wrapped around his shoulders to try to contain the shudders that racked him.

'Several of us did,' he confirmed. 'The old man was the retired headmaster who'd taken over again when the younger man had been conscripted. He was too frail to do anything very physical but he showed us the grating where we could get down into the cellar.' With her head against his chest she could hear his heart pounding as he relived the events, the heat pouring off him as though he was once again lifting each of the children up through the opening to be pulled clear by one of his comrades.

'Then there was only one little girl left. Her name was Oksana…the same as my sister. She was one of the refugee children and had seen so much horror that she was too terrified to come near me, and by the time I got her to trust me, the shelling had begun again.

'We got her out, but when they tried to hurry her away, she refused to leave me, so when the next shell landed, scoring a direct hit on the school, she was blown off her feet. I found out, later, that she landed some long way away in the headmaster's vegetable garden, completely un-injured. I was almost blown out of the hole, coming out of the cellar like toothpaste out of a tube and expecting the whole building to collapse on me at any minute. Unfortunately, the impact on the school had been the final straw for the old boiler and it exploded, sending me cartwheeling in the air before landing with half the school on top of me.'

'So that's why your colleagues were so sure

that you'd died,' she murmured with a shudder of her own for the realisation of exactly how close he'd come to losing his life.

'And they couldn't afford to hang around to find all the pieces, not with all those injured people depending on them,' he said, resignation in his tone. 'The idea of a unit taking their comrades home with them, dead or alive, is a good one, but not if it means risking more lives, and that's what they would have been doing if they had stopped to shift half a school to find me.'

'So, how *did* you survive?'

'Apparently, the boiler ended up saving my life, because it blew the chimney stack over in almost one complete piece, and that ended up holding most of the rest of the debris off me…enough that it was fairly simple to uncover me without doing any further damage. I was still barely conscious when some people in uniform arrived, ready to finish the job the explosion had started on me in spite of the old schoolmaster's objections. If I hadn't spoken in the local dialect, they probably would have done just that.'

'Instead, you told them they were giving you a headache,' she chuckled, remembering what he'd said before. That reminded her of something else he'd said.

'What did you mean, earlier?' She broke the silence that had been weaving itself almost comfortably around them and peered up into his face, wishing that there was just a little more light to be able to see him properly.

'What did *what* mean?' She saw the dark slashes of his eyebrows draw together in a puzzled frown.

'You said something about dreaming about me even when you didn't know who I was. What did you mean by that?'

She didn't need a bright light to see the discomfort appear in his expression and for a moment was certain that he would refuse to explain. Then, suddenly, there was a new determination in the set of his jaw and her heart lifted with the realisation that he wasn't going to fob her off this time.

'It was after the explosion,' he said, the rough edge to his voice telling her that the memories of that time were still raw. 'At first,

I just hurt too much and was too terrified that whichever faction had found me was going to finish the job off to worry about how many injuries I had.

'Then, once I realised that they weren't going to kill me—that they actually wanted to help me—I began to realise how badly hurt I was.' He drew in a shuddering breath that was her only clue to just how much of the detail he was leaving out. 'It was only when they got me to the nearest hospital…a place not much bigger than a small GP surgery and with virtually no equipment or supplies left, due to the ongoing conflict surrounding it…that I realised how much trouble I was in, especially as I couldn't remember where I was, what I was doing there or even who I was.'

'Was it difficult to make yourself understood; to explain that you were a doctor and knew what was wrong with you?' How she was managing to ask a reasonably intelligent question when she was still reeling from that shocking revelation, she didn't know.

'I had no difficulty communicating—once my ears stopped ringing from the explosion—because they were speaking the language I grew up with…although I probably shouldn't be telling you that for reasons of operational security.'

'You mean, they'd sent you back into your own country; to the place you were born?' She couldn't imagine how difficult that would have been for him. From the little he'd told her about his disastrous childhood, it couldn't have been a place he'd been eager to re-visit.

'To a different area,' he corrected her, 'but close enough that they still spoke the same dialect, thank goodness, because that's what saved my life. That, and the children,' he added wryly.

'Were you able to do anything to treat yourself, or did you have to explain what needed doing to the local doctor?'

'What local doctor?' he said wearily. 'The only medical services available to anybody in the area were an elderly midwife with no formal qualifications and one of the local girls who'd been part-way through her training as a nurse when her mother had been killed and she had to come back home to take care of her younger brothers and sisters. The doctor had been marched away at gunpoint in the middle of the night several months earlier, and no-one had seen him since.'

Olivia was almost afraid to ask what treatment he had—or hadn't—received for his injuries, but he didn't wait for her to voice the questions teeming inside her head.

'Between them, Lena and Mariska managed to clean me up and stitch the worst of the gashes…without anaesthetic,' he added in a grimaced aside, 'and they did a good job of setting my arm—using strips of wood for splints, moss for padding and lengths of fabric to bind it all together—but there wasn't much they could do for my legs.'

And suddenly, when the question was there, on the very tip of her tongue, Olivia couldn't make herself ask.

Cowardice had never been something she'd succumbed to, but all the time she didn't have to confront the full details of the damage that had been done to his back and his legs, somehow she could pretend to herself that it was something from which he could recover; that one day, in the not too distant future, he would be standing tall and straight, the same Gregor she'd met and fallen in love with.

And perhaps a selfish tiny part of her didn't

want to know just how little time she would have him to herself; to have him lying in their bed with her arms around him and talking in the quiet shadows of the night.

'I'd better let you rest so the painkillers can get to work…so you can get some sleep,' she murmured, straightening up to put her feet on the floor even as she regretted leaving the warmth and comfort of his arms and walking away.

'Don't go,' he said, then instantly contradicted himself. 'No. You need to sleep, too. The drugs will probably help me to sleep deeply enough that the nightmare can't come back.' But he didn't sound certain, and she was sure that she heard dread in his voice.

'I could stay…just until you fall asleep,' she offered, hoping she didn't sound as pathetically eager as she felt. She hadn't had time to process the ramifications of the fact that Gregor had suffered from traumatic amnesia; was only too willing to excuse him for not contacting her without having any idea just how long the condition had persisted.

How pathetic did that make her?

She had every right to be angry with him for

not trying to get in contact with her as soon as he'd arrived back in Britain. She wouldn't have ended up in the embarrassing position of having to cancel a wedding in front of hundreds of prominent guests if she'd had some kind of warning that her husband was still alive.

But…all she had to do was remember the sound of the pain and despair in his voice when he'd been calling out and she knew that she couldn't leave him to go through that alone.

That's if he really wanted her to sit with him?

There was no reason why he would, given that he'd stayed away so long. He must have had a reason why he hadn't contacted her, and the fact that he'd asked to stay in the flat *could* just be for the sake of convenience or because he couldn't stand being hospitalised any longer.

'Please, stay.' His whispered words were so soft that if she hadn't been listening for them—hoping against hope that he would say them—she might not have heard them at all.

Gregor was exhausted, but for the first time in far longer than he cared to remember, he felt good about it.

For nearly two years he'd welcomed whatever drugged oblivion he'd been able to achieve each night, just to escape from the misery of his existence.

Now he couldn't care less that it was already several hours past the time he could have taken his next dose of analgesia. Hopefully, that meant that the increased level of pain brought on by the rigorous testing he'd undergone was beginning to diminish to a more manageable level.

Anyway, the last thing he wanted to do was move when he had Livvy curled up against his side with her arm laid protectively across him and her hand spread over his heart.

He'd never imagined, when he'd asked her to stay with him, that she would agree to stretch out on the bed beside him instead of sitting up in the chair, still less that she would have accepted his invitation to slide her cold feet under the covers and curl up beside him to share the warmth. He'd hardly dared to breathe when he'd realised that she was drifting off to sleep, revelling in the delight of having her in the bed beside him…albeit with several chaste inches between them.

And if he never told her that he'd waited until

she was sound asleep before he'd taken the chance to coax her into his arms, she'd never know that she hadn't been the one to gravitate towards him the way she'd always done when they were in bed together.

When he'd been lying in the primitive remains of that once-proud little hospital, all but naked and feeling as if every bone in his body had been broken, it had been hard to believe that a day would come when he would welcome the long hours of darkness.

For so long, each day had been something to endure, with no prospect of the damnable mists that clouded his memory ever lifting enough for him to find out who he was and where he belonged.

But at this precise moment, he knew without a shadow of a doubt that he was exactly where he wanted to be—in a warm comfortable bed and with the one woman in the world who meant absolutely everything to him wrapped around him as closely as ivy around a tree trunk.

What might happen when Livvy woke up and found herself here with him, he had no idea, but in the meantime, he had every intention of enjoying the time he *did* have with her.

Time to feel again the familiar weight of her against his side, aware with every molecule of the soft soughing of her warm breath against the curve of his neck, feeling the catch of her silky hair tangling on his emerging stubble and breathing in the soft, utterly female scent of her that surrounded him.

Then he had to stifle a groan of agony as his body responded in a reassuringly male way to those thoughts, having to suppress the fear that he might never be able to do anything to assuage needs that had already been in abeyance for two long years…and that was even if the current uncertain state of their relationship didn't preclude it.

'Gregor?'

The sleep-hazy murmur of her voice emerging from somewhere under his chin told him that she was more asleep than awake and he deliberately kept quiet in the hope that she would go back to sleep again; that he would have a little longer to savour the pleasures of having her in his arms.

The new day was barely starting to break with only the slightest hint of sunrise lightening the darkness, but neither of them had ever been the sort to lie in bed when there was work to be done, their internal clocks fine-tuned during the long years of training to wake them when it was time to get up.

Once upon a time, this had been one of their favourite times to indulge in fast and furious love-making, their passion only seeming to be heightened by the fact that they had to have one eye on the clock to get to work on time.

Today was very different. Neither of them had any pressing reason to leap up and get going. Livvy had probably booked herself at least a fortnight's break for her honeymoon with the Honourable-Baronet-in-waiting, while he…

Well, he had absolutely nowhere he had to be, even if he were capable of getting there…at least, until he made another appointment at the hospital.

A change in the pattern of Livvy's breathing told him that this precious time with her was about to end. Then she stretched like a cat, arching her back and making that sweet mewing sound that had fascinated him from the first time he'd heard it.

She rubbed her cheek against his shoulder, obviously still more asleep than awake, and it was almost as if the intervening years had never happened. The sound in her throat deepened almost to a purr when her position draped across him told her of his body's all-too-eager reaction to her presence, but when he expected… dreaded…the moment she would realise exactly what she was doing…anticipated the way she would shoot backwards across the bed to break any contact, probably with a glare of accusation skewering him to the mattress…he was stunned into speechlessness when none of that happened.

Instead, he was being drawn into an almost dream-like state that was eerily similar to the dreams he'd woven around his mystery woman when he'd hovered between nightmare and agony. Only this time he wasn't imagining gentle hands exploring his body, tracing every dip and hollow, winnowing through the dark hair as she teased her way from one exquisitely sensitive nipple to the other, then following the trail down his quivering body.

He was half-afraid to slide his hands up from her waist to draw the solitary item of clothing over her head, convinced that losing it would bring her to her senses, but when the air swirled around the soft pink globes of her breasts to tighten the deep rose of her nipples into demanding nubs, instead of beating a hasty retreat, she instinctively tried to satisfy her body's demands by undulating her body over his.

His own body was so tightly wound from a combination of years of abstinence and the fear that this unexpected pleasure would be snatched from him—the way it always was when he woke from his dreams—that the first touch of her questing hand at his waistband almost broke his control.

'Livvy!' he growled, certain she must be able to hear the agony of anticipation so clear in his voice. He could have wept when she immediately froze, lifting her head to look down into his face.

Then he saw the expression on her face…her darkly dilated pupils and the way they focused so intently on his mouth.

'Please… I'm sorry, but…may I kiss you?'

Her stumbling request robbed him of any words to answer, but he didn't need words. All he needed to do was reach up to frame her face in his hands and guide her towards him, every molecule in his body taut with expectation.

It was like the first time he'd kissed her—the ripple of fierce sensation that had scythed through him at the first touch of his lips on hers…the fierce possessive heat that had flared through him as he spread his hands open on her back, pulling her closer…and the jolt of disbelief when he heard his own groan, deep and low, its rumble vibrating right through his body, and her softer whimper confirming that she shared the same overwhelming desire.

Yes, this was like that first time—the jolt of total awareness, the firestorm of heat, the visceral desire, but, oh, so much more overwhelming this time because, even though he hadn't known the name of the woman in his dreams, he'd known for two long years exactly what he'd been missing.

'Gregor…no!' she gasped, and he stifled a groan of agony as she tried to disentangle herself from him. 'We can't…you can't…' she panted. 'You're injured.'

'But you're not,' he countered, guiding her mouth back to his.

For several endless seconds she did little more than meekly accept the evocative thrust of his tongue into the dark sweetness of her mouth, then, to his everlasting relief, she suddenly dispensed with any delaying tactics.

In seconds, it seemed, she had both of them naked and their bodies joined in the way he'd been dreaming of for so long. And it was even better than in his dreams…hotter, faster and so very much more explosive, leaving both of them panting as though at the end of a race but with infinitely more pleasure lingering as they relaxed into a familiar post-coital fugue.

Gregor had no idea how long they slept… hadn't had any intention of sleeping at all while he had that soft, lithe, achingly familiar body sprawled bonelessly over the top of his.

Unfortunately, he'd been woken by the gnawing pain that settled into the base of his spine whenever he lay too long on his back—the pain that had driven him to take the first available appointment for a surgical consultation, even though it had been at Livvy's hospital—the pain that, after the events of the night that had just passed, somehow seemed a little less unbearable.

Even so, much as he didn't want to disturb

her—or want to lose the precious head-to-toe contact between their bodies—he was forced to try to slide Olivia to one side.

CHAPTER FIVE

'GREGOR... What...? Oh...! I'm s-sorry,' she stammered when he roused her in spite of his efforts. 'I—I meant to go...not to fall asleep... I should have left...'

'Shh,' he whispered, unbearably tempted to banish her endearing embarrassment with a kiss, but knowing that a single kiss would never be enough...never *had* been enough...and with the level of his pain escalating, he really wasn't in a fit state to do anything about it, even if she were to do most of the work. 'I have no complaints over the fact that you stayed...nor any regrets,' he added.

'You don't?' He wondered if she had any idea how enticing the dawning look of hope in her eyes could be.

'No, Livvy, I don't,' he said firmly. 'My only regret is that I need to move; that I need to take my tablets and visit the bathroom, preferably in very quick succession.'

The reminder that he might need her help to achieve the simplest and most basic of tasks was enough to have her switch instantly into carer mode, much to his disappointment.

If he hadn't been watching her closely, he wouldn't have recognised that it was only a cover for her discomposure over what they'd done during the night, so much so that she was hardly able to look at him as she pulled on the oversized T-shirt she'd flung off in the half-light of the night, tugging in vain at the hem of it to try to cover those mile-long legs.

He didn't know whether to smile at her unexpected embarrassment or groan aloud at the vivid mental images of those legs straddling his body as she rose above him in all her slender naked glory, but he certainly didn't want her to regret what had happened. The last thing he wanted was for her to avoid him when his only chance of sorting the situation out between them was to spend as much time as possible with her…in or out of their bed.

'Thank you, Livvy,' he said quietly when she

silently positioned the chair beside the bed, obviously still searching for some innocuous topic
of conversation to break the uncomfortable
silence, and she blinked, clearly confused.

'You're welcome,' she responded automatically, then a quick frown pinched her eyebrows
together. 'What for?' she demanded warily and
he wondered if her thoughts had been as discom-
forting…and as arousing…as his.

'That was the best night's sleep I've had in
nearly two years,' he said honestly, wondering if
he was doing the right thing to try to side-track
both their minds off the unexpected explosion of
passion between them. 'I don't usually manage
more than a couple of hours—between the painkillers and the nightmares. Then I end up spending
my days feeling as if I haven't slept at all.'

'Could you have slept better because your pain
is less than it was—because the analgesia the
hospital gave you is dealing with it more effec-
tively—or was it because you told me about
what had happened to you…about what happens
in your nightmares?'

He shook his head. 'Talking about it usually
brings the nightmares back worse than ever, and

even though the pain's subsided to its usual level and I'm on different painkillers, I still need them…much as I wish it weren't so,' he admitted, glad to see that, even though she'd retreated behind her medical persona, at least she was looking at him, now.

'Actually…' He paused, suddenly remembering that he might not have time to approach the situation between them slowly. All he could do was hope that he wasn't saying too much too soon and that she wouldn't misunderstand if he didn't find the right words. He didn't really have any other option. Without knowing just how long she was going to let him stay with her, he was going to have to grab every opportunity as it presented itself. 'Apart from…anything else that happened, I think the reason why I slept so well was because you were there with me.'

'Oh.' He saw her eyes widen, her immediate unguarded response a mixture of embarrassment and pleasure, but when her mouth parted as though she might argue the point, all he could imagine was the taste of those soft pink lips. 'Well…um…'

Livvy never had known how to take a compliment, even an implied one, and he'd always blamed her mother's never-ending dissatisfaction with a daughter who'd never meekly given-in to her grandiose plans; her bright, beautiful, loving daughter who'd deserved so much more than to be married off to the highest title Phyllida Mannington-Forbes could find.

But, then, his Livvy had also deserved far better than a man with no family and no country—an orphaned immigrant whose job had meant he was away more than he was with her—but he'd never stopped counting his blessings since she'd accepted his proposal and become his wife.

'So…which do you want, Gregor…the bathroom or painkillers?' She was trying to be efficient and impersonal but he wondered if she was aware just how much her expression had softened.

'Do I have to choose?' he dared to tease. 'Can't I have both—please?'

Gregor's attempt at a joke had lightened the mood enough for the two of them to be able to deal with the list of routine basic necessities from getting him out of bed to seeing him fully dressed and sitting at the table, but Olivia found it harder and harder to maintain her well-practised doctor's composure with each new look at the scars on his battered body.

As far as she could tell, the various surgical incisions had healed well, but there was clear evidence that he'd had a small forest of sutures at one time or another, and as for the oldest scars— the lasting evidence of the jagged, ragged injuries that must have confronted those two women when he'd first been brought to the impoverished hospital—it was a wonder that he'd survived long enough to have the later corrective surgeries.

How he'd ever survived such extensive injuries without being overwhelmed by infection, she'd never know. He'd already told her that the hospital had been ill equipped, so there would have been no access to the sort of antibiotics he should have had, nor any blood to replace the volume he would have lost from that degree of trauma.

As for his most recent visit to hospital…had that just been a formality, to check that everything that had been done for him had healed properly? Was it just a case of punishing physical rehabilitation and time, now, before he

regained a workable level of mobility and independence, or was there more gruelling surgery
waiting for him in the near future?

She was desperate to know exactly what the
surgeons had done to him and what prognosis
they had given him, but she knew how important
it was to bite her tongue for the moment.
Frustrating as it was, she knew that the man
she'd married would find it hard to deal with any
more detailed conversation about the state of his
health until *he* was ready to initiate it.

That didn't mean that they were going to be
able to avoid the conversation indefinitely, she
decided silently. In fact, as soon as breakfast was
over and tidied away, she would make certain
that she kept him in the hot seat until she had at
least some of the answers she needed.

In the meantime, it was all too easy to slip
back into the easy familiarity that had charac-
terised their relationship right from the beginning. In spite of the passion that had sparked
between them from the first time they had met,
and had only grown more potent as they had
come to know and trust each other more
deeply, there had been a strangely comfort-

able sense of companionship that had been as effortless as if they had always known each other.

With her decision to talk after the meal banishing the tension inside her, their conversation over the breakfast table was as normal and far-ranging as if the intervening two years had never happened.

In fact, Olivia was just beginning to allow herself to hope that there was a completely logical explanation for everything that had happened— to believe that their life could be put back together as though she hadn't spent nearly two years believing that he was gone for ever—when the phone pealed out its strident summons.

'Leave it,' Gregor growled, his dark brows suddenly drawn together into a sharp angle above that unexpectedly elegant nose. 'Let the machine answer it.'

'I certainly don't want word to get back to my mother that I'm here. She'd probably arrive within the hour,' she agreed, pulling a face then feeling guilty that she should be so loath to speak to her own parent.

She knew that her mother and father cared about her, in their own slightly detached way, but she was absolutely sick of her mother's need to micromanage her only child's life.

'Olivia…this is Ash,' the familiar cultured voice announced, and when she saw the way tension suddenly sent Gregor's shoulders rigid, tightening his hands into fists and pouring out of him in almost-visible waves, she wondered if it might have been better to risk taking the call after all.

'If you're there, old girl, this is just a friendly warning that your mother will probably be turning up on your doorstep.' She could hear the grimace in his voice, calm as it sounded as he continued.

'Someone has apparently sold the tabloids the story of the wedding that never was. Their blood-hounds have found out that you're not at the honeymoon hotel after all, and came back to both sets of parents with the information demanding to know where you're hiding out. Your mother's convinced herself that you would never have just set off for anywhere else for a fortnight without taking the time to plan it properly—the way she would—so it would probably be wise to get out of her way for a few days if you don't want her company.'

Olivia shuddered at the image *that* presented. Luckily, her mother was far too conscious of the 'right' way to behave to have a screaming fit in the middle of several hundred of her closest aristocratic friends, but the gloves would come off with a vengeance if she ever had Gregor cornered somewhere private. And the fact that he was in a wheelchair and physically unable to escape her excoriating tongue wouldn't be likely to make her soften her attack, either. When it came to protecting her family's position in society, Phyllida Mannington-Forbes's killer's instinct for the jugular was far too highly developed.

'If you're *really* away…' The pause on the tape went on so long that she began to wonder if the connection had been broken till she clearly heard the sound of another voice in the background—a male voice—and Ash hurried to end the call with a flippant, 'Well, if you've really gone away somewhere, good for you. Take care of yourself. Bye, old girl.'

Olivia had been facing Gregor when the message had started and when she saw his expression change, had been overcome with a terrible feeling of guilt—almost as if she'd deliberately set out to betray him with Ash.

She had to remind herself that *he* had been the

one who'd left her, not the other way around. It had been for work, admittedly, and he'd had no option, but Gregor certainly hadn't bothered hurrying to get in touch when he'd returned to the UK. And he *still* hadn't explained why.

His grey eyes were stormy in the aftermath of the message, but she could still decipher a strange mixture of anger and frustration in them as she tried to get her own thoughts in some sort of order to start that all-important conversation.

It had only been a matter of hours since she'd heard his voice coming from the back of the church—less than a day—but already she could feel her resolve being weakened in exactly the same way as it had when she'd first met the man and fallen in love with him, in spite of her determination that she would complete her training before she allowed herself to be side-tracked by any man.

She'd known right from the moment she'd applied for a place at medical school that she would only have one chance at forcing her mother to accept her desire to train as a doctor. Any sign that she wasn't whole-heartedly focused on that goal and Phyllida would have taken it that her exasperating daughter had only been using the excuse of training for a profession as a means of delaying the day when she would meekly accept her mother's choice of the perfect husband.

Well, her overwhelming attraction towards Gregor had blind-sided her once, but she'd had two long years to school herself into controlling her emotions, good and bad, and she wasn't going to make that mistake again.

This time, if there was going to be any sort of relationship between them, it wasn't going to be forged in the crucible of their passion for each other. She had a powerful and well-trained brain that found it easy to sift through a patient's disparate symptoms to arrive at a diagnosis, only this time she was going to step back and allow it time to weigh everything up so that she could decide whether there was any point in letting herself be vulnerable again.

'Gregor, we need to talk—' she started in a rush.

'Livvy, I don't think this is going to work—' he began, at exactly the same time as the phone began to ring again.

Impatiently, Gregor muttered something under his breath and suddenly Olivia was catapulted back to an earlier time, the first time she'd heard him speaking the language he'd learned as a child.

She'd been fascinated by the sound of it and by the way his accent carried over more strongly into the first few sentences when he switched back to English, the slightly rough, yet liquid edge to the words affecting something deep inside her.

She was instantly wrapped up in her usual game of trying to work out whether he really was swearing or if his angry words just *sounded* that way; so distracted that she found herself automatically reaching her hand out towards the imperious ring of the phone.

'Don't!' he reminded her, sharply, and she waited for the machine to take over.

'Oh, no, it's one of those wretched answering-machines,' said an unknown female voice when the machine finally cut in. 'Are you sure this is the right number, Staff Nurse? Should I leave a message…just in case it's the right place?'

There was the muffled sound of an indecipherable reply somewhere in the background then the voice returned to begin again.

'Ok... Here goes... This is a message for Gregor Davidov, recently an orthopaedic patient at this hospital. Please, can you tell him to contact the orthopaedic surgery department urgently and ask for Mr d'Agostino's secretary to make a follow-up appointment for the rest of his tests? Oh...or please contact us to tell us if you know how to contact him if he's not at this number, or to let us know if we've got the wrong number entirely,' she added in a garbled afterthought before the connection was broken.

There was an uncomfortable silence in the room when the call ended and Olivia knew that Gregor was waiting to see whether she was going to confront him for being so presumptuous when he'd registered with the hospital, albeit with the original version of his name rather than the one they shared.

In truth, for a moment it was a toss-up whether she would point out that he hadn't asked permission to give the hospital her telephone number as his contact point without so much as a by-your-leave, or whether she was going to tear strips off him because he hadn't told her that he would be needing an urgent appointment with the orthopaedic consultant.

For him to disappear out of her life for nearly two years only to reappear with every expectation that he would be welcome to take up residence in their flat was presumptuous in the extreme, especially when he'd made absolutely no attempt to warn her…or even to inform her that he was alive and back in the country.

The fact that the voice on the phone had referred to Gregor as Davidov rather than Davidson barely registered in comparison with the importance of one of the hospital's most senior consultants leaving a message about an urgent appointment. And what were these tests that he was supposed to be having?

It was no surprise to her that he'd chosen to make his appointment at the hospital where she worked because, having worked there himself, Gregor knew at first hand just how highly their orthopaedic department was rated. She could only suppose that his use of the original spelling of his name had been an attempt at preventing her from knowing that he was there, but the reason *why* he hadn't wanted her to know was one of the questions she still had to ask him.

As for his physical condition…well, the questions just seemed to be multiplying.

Was Gregor treating his health negligently by signing himself out the way he had? Was his condition worsening because the injuries hadn't been properly treated in the first place or was there a chance that another operation could improve matters for him? To her frustration, she had absolutely no idea because he hadn't yet told her any details about the severity of his condition, but the tone of that phone message certainly sounded as if someone at the hospital was seriously concerned about him.

Her pulse rate must have doubled, at least, but it felt as if her blood had frozen in her veins when she thought about the damage he could have done to himself…the damage *she* could have done to him by hauling him in and out of the wheelchair without knowing whether it was safe to do so, and as for that explosive interlude this morning…well, the fact that she'd been the aggressor…that *she'd* been the dominant one who should have used her position of power to stop anything happening…

An overwhelming feeling of guilt had her ready to explode at him as she stalked towards him, ashamed that she was intending to use the fact that she could tower over him for the first time in their relationship to enforce her point.

'Gregor, tell me you didn't—' she began, but the phone rang again and she gave a shriek of frustration, tempted to rip the wire out of the wall if that was the only way she could vent her anger at the constant interruptions.

'Olivia, this is Tricia and I hope you're not going to hate me for ever, but it's all round the grapevine that you didn't get married after all— and I shall be expecting the full skinny about that the first free moment we get—but I'm really hoping that means that you're at a loose end and can come in to cover Tony's shift. He and Duncan were on their way to play in the hospital's rugby team and were sideswiped by a drunk on a roundabout…drunk at this time of the morning, for heaven's sake!' her colleague added in a typical aside. 'Anyway, he's got a broken leg—comminuted fracture, of course; Tony never does anything by halves—and is on his way up to Theatre to have it pinned. Oh, and

Dunc's too bruised and shaken to be any use to anyone, today. So give me a ring as soon as you get this message…*please*! Better still, turn up as soon as you can. It's bedlam here.'

Suddenly, a whole row of jigsaw pieces slotted neatly into place in Livvy's head, and instead of returning to the ear-bashing she'd intended giving Gregor she whirled and made her way towards the other end of the flat.

'What are you doing?' Gregor's voice was so close behind her that she knew he was following her. Well, *good*; that would save her from shouting.

'Packing,' she said shortly.

'What? Why?' He could be a man of few words sometimes, and this was obviously one of them.

She had the feeling that when he'd wheeled his chair into the bedroom he'd deliberately positioned himself right in her way between the wardrobe and the small bag she'd placed open on the bed. 'I understand that you want to help them at the hospital, but what will *I* do?' he demanded.

'You're going with me,' she said shortly, briskly manoeuvring the chair out of her way and continuing to pick from the neat piles of 'everyday' bras and pants she'd left behind in the top drawer and moving on to the neat row of trousers and blouses that were her self-imposed uniform for going to work. She hadn't expected to need to retrieve any of them until she returned from her honeymoon.

'Going where?' He didn't get in her way this time, but his tone of voice was every bit as much of a demand for her attention as his previous position had been.

'We're *both* going to the hospital,' she clarified as she swiftly added a handful of items from the top of the dressing table while she tried to think where the rest of her wash-kit could have gone. She had the little emergency bag with the miniature versions of her favourite soap, shampoo and toothpaste, but the fancy waterproof one that had enough room for the full-sized containers and her cosmetics, too, seemed to be missing.

Belatedly, she remembered that it was packed away in the luggage that had been destined for her honeymoon, still stacked neatly just inside the front door, courtesy of Parker.

'And while I'm getting things together, you

can phone Rick d'Agostino's secretary and get her to sign you back in so you're ready for those tests and that appointment.'

'No.' It was only one word but it was as harsh and forceful as anything he'd ever said to her, evidence of how strongly he meant his refusal. 'I'm not going into hospital again.'

Frustration nearly made her explode, but she'd had long years of practice in dealing with her mother and managed to hang on to her control.

'Obviously, that's your decision to make, but take it from me, top orthopaedic consultants of Rick d'Agostino's calibre don't routinely have their secretaries phone patients to invite them to make urgent appointments.' She drew in a steadying breath to ensure that her voice wouldn't rise and spoil the illusion of calm…in through her nose while she counted up to five and then out equally slowly through her pursed lips before she continued in as reasonable tone as she could manage.

'Still, if you'd rather stay here by yourself, be my guest, but I'll be leaving in about ten minutes. I'm taking Ash's warning seriously, so I'm not hanging around to welcome my mother.

Give her my love when you see her…if she ever lets you get a word in edgeways.'

'Livvy…!' The mixture of emotions contained in that one word would have been enough to make her cave in two years ago, especially as she knew he wasn't the sort of man to cope with helplessness easily. But she was dealing with overwhelming emotions, here, too, and her need to take care of this man…to honour the part of her vows that had spelled out her responsibilities towards him in sickness and in health…was paramount when she still had no idea of the severity of his condition.

'Make up your mind, Gregor,' she said, hoping she sounded resolute enough to convince him, even though most of her attention was focused on trying to guess what sort of tests Rick d'Agostino wanted to perform so urgently. 'Are you going to make that phone call before I drive us both to the hospital, or do I leave you here?'

She stalked across the room to the second set of wardrobes and heard his sharply indrawn breath when she opened the door to reveal the fact that his belongings were still there, untouched from the day she'd neatly hung his freshly ironed 'civilian' shirts away the day after he'd left on that last posting.

Her face was burning at this mute evidence that she'd never really believed that he was never coming back to her; that she hadn't been able to force herself to dispose of anything that belonged to the man she'd loved, even though he'd officially been declared dead.

Gregor stared in disbelief at the neat array of suits and shirts, his heart suddenly beating so fast that he could hardly breathe.

He hadn't even bothered to open the wardrobe doors that morning to see if he had something other than the rather crumpled borrowed clothing that had been left in his soft-sided holdall all night; hadn't even considered that Livvy might have kept his things when he'd been away for so long.

But she *had* kept them.

In fact, it looked as if she'd kept every-thing…even the disreputable old leather jacket that he'd bought for himself with his first earnings as a teenager. It might even fit him, at last, now that heaving himself around had built up the muscles in his shoulders and arms. It would certainly fit him better than it had when he'd bought it large enough to wear several bulky layers underneath it, the habit of buying clothing big enough to allow for growth something he'd always found hard to break.

But the fact that she'd even kept that scruffy jacket wasn't what was important. What really mattered was the reason *why* Livvy hadn't thrown everything away…or, at least, donated it to some good cause.

He now knew that it had been nearly two years since she'd been informed that he'd died in that explosion and the fact that she'd been just seconds away from marrying that perfect upper-crust fashion plate was evidence enough that she'd moved on, emotionally, so why hadn't she done the most logical thing and got rid of the clutter he'd left behind him?

Just the thought of the recent phone call from her would-be husband stirred something deep inside him. His honest recognition that the man was a far better match for Livvy didn't stop a low growl of frustration building up in the back of his throat and he could almost feel himself turning into a knuckle-dragging Neanderthal.

'What's your decision?'

The crisp question could easily have come from his former commanding officer rather than his wife, he mused wryly as he wheeled himself across to the wardrobe and gave in to the inevitable.

'Can you grab a couple of shirts for me, please?' he asked, even as she was reaching over his head to take out a handful of hangers and surrounding him with the scent of vanilla and spice that had haunted him for the last two years. He refused to allow the fact that he'd been unable to reach the shirts for himself to darken his mood still further, opting instead to pull several tracksuits from a shelf before pulling open the drawer that he knew would still hold neat stacks of underwear and socks.

There was a strange comfort in knowing that their shared love of order and organisation didn't seem to have changed in the time they'd been apart, he mused in the silence of the taxi a few minutes later, but that would be far too little on which to start rebuilding their relationship.

And that was always supposing that Livvy was interested in rebuilding it, he thought darkly, deliberately shutting out the claustrophobic sensation that surrounded him as soon as he entered the main reception area of the hospital.

Then, of course, there was his appointment with Rick d'Agostino.

Just the thought of it was enough to send his stomach plunging towards his feet, and that, combined with the swift ascent of the lift, left him feeling distinctly light-headed.

'What time are you due to see the consultant?' Livvy asked with a quick glance at her watch.

'You haven't got time to sit around with me waiting for an appointment,' he said hurriedly. 'You're needed down in A and E. Urgently, remember?'

She was clearly torn, the caring side of her nature wanting to stay with him so that he had some company while he waited, but to his relief, her responsible side won out.

'Trish did sound a bit frazzled, with two members of staff missing,' she agreed. 'Are you sure you don't mind if I go?'

He reassured her that he was unlikely to be kept waiting long, and then was astounded to find himself tempted to call her back when he saw her walking away, suddenly feeling a great wave of the same unutterable loneliness that had weighed him down while he'd lain in that far-away hospital bed convinced he would die without even knowing his real name.

'Gregor. Good…good! I am pleased you could come in so quickly,' Rick d'Agostino said as he strode swiftly towards him, the grey streaks in his curly hair almost looking like sparks of electricity, the man seemed so full of energy. 'Let us go through to repeat that last set of nerve-conduction tests, then we will talk. Yes?'

Sick dread had settled like lead in the pit of Gregor's stomach along with the realisation that it was all very well making plans to persuade Livvy to let him back into her life again for good, but until he knew the results of all the tests he'd undergone, he didn't know whether he would have any sort of quality of life to offer to share with her.

To think that he'd once taken his health and strength for granted. He'd never had the slightest problem in passing his annual fitness test, completing his required push-ups, sit-ups and run with time to spare. Now, he would barely be able to get to the start line and out of his chair before the test was over.

And the last thing he would ever do was condemn her to be his caretaker and nurse for the rest of his life. *That* was the fundamental reason he'd delayed letting her know that he was alive. He'd been desperate to see her, but almost equally determined that he would return to her on his own two feet or not at all. Only his discovery of her imminent marriage had put paid to that plan.

So, he was having to take things one day at a time, and if he was revelling in spending even a few extra hours in her company, well, he would have to see that as an unexpected bonus.

'You weren't joking, were you?' Olivia exclaimed when she caught her first sight of the crammed board, her preoccupation with the lonely image Gregor had made when she'd left him waiting for his appointment pushed to the back of her mind.

'You should know by now that I never joke about needing extra sets of hands,' Trish said crisply. 'Now, Livvy—darling, please tell me you've come prepared to work a full shift at twice the speed of light.'

Olivia laughed. 'I live to serve,' she said. 'So, where do you want me to start?'

'I might need to grab you if we have more than one thing at a time come in to majors, but if you could start with the cubicles...?' Trish suggested.

'To hear is to obey.' Olivia sketched an obsequious bow then squared her shoulders and set off for the first patient, as ever looking forward to doing what she saw as one of the most interesting jobs in the hospital. Where else could a doctor have a surprise behind every curtain and a different set of problems with every patient?

CHAPTER SIX

IT TOOK Olivia several hours before she felt as if she was starting to make some headway, or perhaps it was just because the early morning rush was tailing off, giving the hospital time to re-group before the afternoon onslaught began.

She'd heard the comings and goings of several traumas arriving at the other end of the department and part of her craved the adrenaline rush that always came with knowing that every second could count if they were to save a seriously injured patient's life. The other part of her was quite grateful to be down at this end where there had been absolutely no time for her colleagues to grill her about the farce her wedding day had become. Not that they hadn't wanted to, she admitted wryly, knowing that she'd deliberately delayed taking a break for just that reason.

Now, though, she was feeling the need to stretch her legs, straighten the kinks out of her neck and back and find herself something to drink. And if that meant that she might be cornered and quizzed, at least she had a chance to deflect questions under the pretext of catching up on what had been happening in the rest of the department.

The last thing she expected was to turn the corner and see Gregor's wheelchair disappearing into one of the rooms further along the corridor.

What on earth was he doing down here? she wondered as she followed on his trail. She could understand if he'd come down to tell her that he'd finished his appointment with Rick d'Agostino, but it was unlikely that he'd be in need of sutures after an outpatient appointment in the orthopaedic department, no matter how urgent. And, anyway, they wouldn't have sent him down to A and E for that.

She arrived in the doorway just in time to hear him introduce himself over the sound of heartbroken sobbing.

'Hey, I'm Dr Gregor and I've been told that you need some help with a jigsaw puzzle.'

The sudden strange silence that greeted his

announcement piqued her interest and she managed to position herself so that she could just see the person he was talking to. Or rather the people, because there were two of them sitting on the bed, obviously mother and daughter from their faces, the little child clutched tightly in her mother's arms.

Both were tearstained but, more pertinently, both were liberally spattered with blood.

'Why are you in that chair?' demanded the wide-eyed little moppet bluntly, clearly fascinated enough by Gregor's mode of transport to stop crying.

'Because my legs got tired and I needed to sit down,' he replied simply, then returned to his original question. 'So, what about this puzzle you need my help with?'

'What puzzle?' The mother's voice was shaky, obviously still affected by whatever had caused their injuries but apparently willing to play along, especially now that her daughter had stopped crying.

'Well, I'm the top person in the hospital for putting things back together so you can hardly see where they were apart, and I was told that there were two people in here that needed me to put them back together really, really neatly.'

'Like a jigsaw?' the youngster asked warily. 'But won't it come apart again?'

'Not the way I do it,' Gregor said confidently. 'Because I'm the best.'

'So, how do you do it?' she demanded cautiously. 'Will it hurt?'

'Not if I'm extra-careful,' he promised. 'And if I have my special helper with me.' He threw a wicked glance over his shoulder and beckoned, and she realised with a sudden spike of awareness that he'd somehow known that she'd been there the whole time. 'Come in, Livvy, and meet my new friends.'

Olivia shivered, wondering exactly *how* he'd known she was there. She was absolutely certain that she hadn't made a sound and neither of his patients had so much as glanced in her direction, and yet *he'd* known.

Surely, it couldn't be that strange sixth sense that had seemed to operate between the two of them, telling each of them when the other was close by? Surely, something like that couldn't have survived the two years they'd been apart?

Her heart lifted inside her when she realised that one thing that certainly hadn't changed was the way the two of them worked together. It was almost as if words were unnecessary…apart from the stream of light-hearted nonsense that kept little Kylie entertained while her wounds were cleaned and debrided then sutured with the finest, neatest stitches she'd ever seen.

'What on earth had happened?' Olivia asked after they left, Kylie sporting two 'I was very brave' stickers on her blood-spattered sparkly pink T-shirt—one for each arm—and her mother clutching a prescription for antibiotics and an instruction sheet.

'The grandmother came to visit, bringing her cat with her,' Gregor explained as he stripped off his disposable gloves and fired them unerringly into the bin. 'Grandmother's cat attacked Kylie's cat, so the little girl tried to separate them and got attacked by both.'

'So, how did you get roped-in to dealing with it?' she asked as she kept pace with his chair on the way to the staffroom and her much-delayed infusion of coffee. A sudden thought struck her. 'When did you have your last painkillers?'

Gregor threw her a dark look. 'Surely you know me better than to think I would treat patients if I was under the influence of analgesia that strong,' he growled. 'As for dealing with some simple suturing…I was here, I was available, and I was ready, willing and able to pitch in, especially as it's something at which I've become rather proficient,' he added as he negotiated a path through the scattering of chairs littering the staffroom.

'Dealing with injured children, or suturing?' she asked, and found herself automatically fixing his coffee without needing to ask him how he wanted it.

'Both,' he said with a shrug. 'Even when I didn't know who I was or where I came from, somehow I still knew that I was a doctor, and once I'd recovered enough to make myself useful…'

He didn't really need to say any more because that was just the way Gregor had always been…incapable of sitting around if there was someone who needed his help.

'But you're not a member of staff here,' she pointed out. 'If someone took it into their head to make a complaint, HR would go ballistic.'

'The A and E consultant contacted the human resources department and told them to get the paperwork sorted by the time he sent me in to see my first patient so that I'd be covered by the hospital's insurance.' He grinned. 'It was amazing to see how fast they arrived with the paperwork to get my signature.'

'It probably helped, the fact that you'd actually worked here during your training. It wouldn't have taken very long to check up that you hadn't been struck off in the meantime. Oh!' A sudden thought struck her. 'I wonder if the computer tried to tell them that you're not alive any more!'

Gregor chuckled aloud, the sound strangely rusty as if he hadn't had much opportunity to laugh since he'd disappeared from her life. 'I wonder if that's why the young woman from HR gave me that funny look? Perhaps she was expecting to see a corpse?'

'So—' she sank gratefully into the nearest chair and kicked her shoes off '—how did your appointment with Rick d'Agostino go?'

If she hadn't been looking for it, she probably wouldn't have seen the way his whole body seemed to grow unnaturally still...almost like prey sensing the presence of a hunter. And yet what possible danger could such a question pose?

Unless…

Unless, after examining all the results, the orthopaedic surgeon had given Gregor bad news at the end of his appointment?

Had he had to tell him that there was little more that could be done for him, surgically or otherwise, or was there something else…?

'It was a relatively short appointment today,' Gregor volunteered, his tone far too casual. 'Just the last of the nerve-conduction tests.'

'So, when will you get the results? Were you given any idea?' Olivia was certain that there was a secret sub-text to this conversation—one to which she hadn't been given the code.

'I've made another appointment for tomorrow morning. Rick's going to fit me in between his other patients,' he said tersely.

It was only when she realised that he must have guessed that she would agree to cover another shift in the morning that she suddenly understood what was going on. Gregor didn't want her to go with him when he went to see the orthopaedic surgeon for the results, so he'd made it as unlikely as possible for her to be able to accompany him without letting her A and E colleagues down.

Gregor felt sick when he saw the way Livvy's expression changed and knew she'd realised that he didn't want her to go with him to his next appointment.

It wasn't true, exactly, because he would love to have her there with him; craved the support he knew she would give unstintingly. But that was also the reason why he *couldn't* have her there, because if it was bad news, he knew she would be determined to stick by him, no matter how disastrous that would be for her own life and happiness.

He couldn't allow that.

The last two years had been hellish, between not knowing who he was and feeling so utterly powerless, but that was nothing compared to the way he felt about the situation now that his memory had returned. He couldn't describe how he felt, being back with Livvy, the love of his life, but if the results tomorrow were bad, there was no way that his pride would let him be a burden on such a giving, caring woman.

Livvy deserved better. She deserved the chance to start a new life with a man who could give her everything she wanted—a whole, healthy husband and the chance to begin the family they'd been talking about starting, just before he'd gone away. She deserved a second chance to marry the man her parents had always known would be the best husband for her.

As for him…he could always go back to the village and the courageous people who had fought to keep him alive even though he'd been a stranger to them. With the compensation he would eventually receive for his injuries, he could do a lot to restore the medical facilities destroyed during the fighting. And even if he was condemned to the wheelchair for the rest of his life, he already knew that he could contribute to repaying his saviours' generosity by passing on his knowledge about piecing people back together.

If only he could manage to do the same for his own life…or, at least, for his heart.

Perhaps he could find some sort of closure for one set of nightmares, at least, if he were to search out the final resting place of the family he'd lost so many years ago. He knew it hadn't been his fault that his parents had died, but Janek and Oksana had been in his care…as their big brother, it had been his responsibility to keep them safe and he'd failed, disastrously. But maybe there was a chance that, if he found their graves and told them how sorry he was that he hadn't been able to protect them, they might stop haunting him.

In the meantime, there were any number of patients waiting for attention and Tricia seemed to be only too willing to cherry-pick the ones he could easily deal with. At least his finely-honed skill with a needle, gained through many pains-taking hours of piecing together the villagers fighting to protect their families, was standing him in good stead.

So, why was it that he could feel so little sat-isfaction when he managed to salvage the face of the pretty girl who'd been an innocent by-stander pushed through a shopfront window during a gang fight? Why was it so hard to ap-preciate the fact that his careful piecing together of the torn muscles in a young motorcyclist's arm would eventually give him the power and mobility he would need to continue to earn his living? Why was it that all he could see replaying in an endless loop inside his head was the hurt in Livvy's eyes when she'd realised that he was shutting her out of his life—again—and knowing that he couldn't tell her why...might never be able to tell her why.

It was the first time in hours that Olivia had managed to find the time to come to the treatment room that had swiftly been dubbed 'Gregor's room', and she found herself smiling when she realised the subtle changes that had already been made to accommodate him.

The hated wheelchair had been relegated to a corner, replaced by a wheeled stool that looked almost as if it had an enlarged bicycle saddle for a seat. The ubiquitous scrubs he was wearing seemed to camouflage the unnatural thinness of his legs, her eyes being drawn, instead, to the impressive muscular width of his shoulders and the teasing glimpse of dark hair in the V of the neckline.

His concentration had been legendary, even when he'd been training, and with his dark head bent towards the latest gruesome laceration highlighted by the bright task light, that obviously hadn't changed.

But it was his hands that she noticed most.

There were a couple of plastic surgeons on staff at the hospital who could equal the perfection of the reconstructive job he was doing, but not one of them could have done it at that impressive speed.

'Did you want me for something…or have you just come to watch me working?' he challenged with an unexpected gleam in those liquid silver eyes as he glanced at her over his shoulder.

Once again he had known she was there, and she knew very well that he realised that she'd been watching him working and cursed her pale skin as she felt the heat of a blush rise up her throat and into her face. She had always loved watching his apparently effortless skill, even during his training, but hoped he had no idea that she'd also spent a fair amount of time just admiring *him*. He glanced up again and the expression in his eyes had the blush deepening when she realised that the answer to both questions was yes.

Yes, she loved watching him work, especially

with the new confidence he'd somehow acquired during the last two years that almost elevated what he was doing to artistry. And, yes, she wanted him; desperately wanted him in every way there was, in spite of the core of anger that still burned deep inside her—justifiable anger that he'd cared so little for her feelings that, as soon as his memory had returned, he hadn't contacted her to let her know he was alive.

'I just came to tell you that Trish says you're to go for your break. Apparently, she's already told you twice and doesn't want to be seen as a nag!'

'Well, I've nearly finished here,' he said as he bent over his work again, his hands working swiftly and surely as he placed the last few stitches in what must have started off as a daunting gash in the silent woman's arm. 'There,' he said in a voice full of satisfaction when the dressing was in place and he straightened up to pull off his gloves. 'They will give you a leaflet with instructions in Reception, Mrs Northam. It will tell you how to take care of your wound and when you should make an appointment with your GP to have the stitches taken out.'

'Can't *you* take them out?' she pleaded softly, and for the first time Olivia really looked at the woman, and the expression in her eyes—an indescribable mixture of desperation and defeat—was something she'd seen far too often before; something that made her blood boil, but before she could say anything, Gregor was speaking.

'I would be delighted to do that for you,' he said gently as he pulled the instrument-laden trolley out of her way to allow her to get to her feet, 'but in return, will you do something for me?'

'Me? Do something for you?' There was a flash of disbelief in her tired eyes as she flicked a glance towards Olivia standing quietly by. 'Well…if I can. What did you want me to do?'

'I would like you to go with Olivia, here, and have a word with the security man outside.'

'S-security?' Now she looked terrified. 'But, I haven't done anything wrong.'

'I know *you* haven't,' he said reassuringly, then fixed her with the sort of steely glare that would have had strong men quaking in their boots. 'But if you don't report the person who did this to you, the next time I see you it might be too late to save your life.'

'Oh, but…I couldn't do that.' She was shaking her head wildly, her eyes as frantic as a hunted animal's searching for a way out of a trap. 'He would kill me if I said anything.'

'Mrs Northam…Iris…he'll kill you anyway, one of these days,' he pointed out bluntly, even though his tone was gentle. 'It doesn't matter what you did or what you said that he used as an excuse to attack you, he *doesn't* have the right to hurt you. No one does. It's only because you were lucky this time that he didn't hit anything major when he took that knife to you.'

'I didn't tell you that.' The pulse at the base of her pale throat was fluttering at twice its normal speed and she was trembling visibly. 'I…I told you. I…I scratched myself…on…on some barbed wire.'

Gregor sat looking at her, a single raised eyebrow telling her without a word being spoken that he knew how her injury had really occurred.

Even though everything in Olivia was prompting her to wrap a supportive arm around the poor downtrodden woman's shoulders, she waited, trusting Gregor's instincts. The tension in the room became so sharp that she found herself holding her breath, her crossed fingers hidden in the pockets of her scrub top.

'Oh, God help me,' the woman wailed suddenly, and tears began to pour down her face. 'I can't b-bear it any more. I'm so f-frightened all the time and he…'

'Shh! Shh!' Finally Olivia could offer her the comfort she needed, settling her back on the trolley when her legs no longer supported her. 'You sit here while I go and fetch a cup of tea.' She handed the box of paper hankies to Gregor on her way out of the door, nodding when he mouthed the word 'police' to her.

It was nearly an hour before the woman police officer escorted Iris Northam out of A and E, all of them having waited until they had confirmation that her brutish husband had been arrested in their blood-spattered kitchen and charged with grievous bodily harm against his wife. Even then, Iris wasn't returning home but was being taken to a women's shelter where there was an expert counsellor waiting to speak with her.

'I will *never* understand,' Gregor said grimly,

the words almost exploding out of him. 'How can a man call himself a man if he will terrorise a defenceless woman like that? He is *less* than an animal.'

Olivia couldn't answer, especially when she knew of old that such questions were sometimes prompted by the memories of some of the dreadful things he had seen when he had been away from her. Perhaps, if he had been allowed to tell her where he'd been and what he'd done—and seen—it would help to banish some of the nightmares...but, then, Gregor's protective nature would probably see the fact that he needed to burden her with such things as a sign of unmanly weakness in himself.

'We're both overdue for something to eat and drink,' she said firmly, sidestepping the topic completely as she brought his wheelchair across to him.

They hadn't even had time to make a decision about which of the unappetising choices they were going to use to refuel themselves for the second half of their shift when pagers started going off in several pockets simultaneously.

'There must be something nasty coming in,' Gregor commented, putting the tray back on the pile when a glance around the room showed a surgical registrar and his corresponding SHO catching up with the CT radiographer and anaesthetist already on their way towards the door.

'You don't need to come,' Olivia said as she switched off her own pager. 'Stay here and get something to eat.' But she may as well have saved her breath. The stubborn man was already sending his chair hurtling towards the nearest bank of lifts.

'What have we got?' she demanded of the nearest member of staff as they reached the majors end of the department, annoyed to find she was considerably more out of breath than Gregor.

'Listen up, everybody,' the A and E consultant called, and the hubbub of voices instantly died away. 'We've got two cars full of kids—mid to late teens. Head-on impact. Luckily, most are walking wounded but there are three coming in on blue lights. One front-seat passenger had the dashboard pushed back onto his legs. Multiple breaks. One rear-seat passenger, not wearing a belt so impacted with the front seat. Broken rib punctured a lung. Third major casualty was only wearing a lap belt and has a step deformity to her spine. It'll be at least another half an hour before they can extricate her safely, but the others are due to start arriving at any minute.'

He didn't really need to say anything more to anyone who'd been working in A and E during the last ten years because they could guess what was coming.

The department was becoming depressingly accustomed to dealing with sudden influxes of injured youngsters. Luckily, most were relatively minor wounds, garnered during drunken brawls, but when powerful cars driven at high speeds were added to the mix, the department could rapidly become so stretched trying to cope with the severity of the injuries that very little could be done for any of the other patients who might need attention.

'Gregor, are you up for another hour or two of sticking and stitching?' called a voice somewhere on the other side of the mêlée of personnel hurrying to their new assignments.

'Of course,' he called back, the deep resonance of his voice carrying easily over the hasty gaggle of conferences as supplies were ordered and the labs and blood bank were given a heads up. 'I'm always up for it,' he added as he threw a wicked glance at Olivia.

She glowered at him, knowing that the rat remembered only too well what that particular phrase, spoken with his own particular husky accent did to her. How many times, in the early days of their marriage, had he said those words just for the pleasure of seeing her blush, knowing that she would be imagining all the ways he could prove the truth of them when they went back to their flat?

'Olivia, you're with me,' directed the A and E consultant briskly. 'Hopefully, between us, we'll have time to stabilise both the chest and the legs and get them transferred elsewhere before they get the spinal injury here.'

'OK,' she agreed automatically, but for a second she stood there, unable to move her feet as she stared after Gregor's back, feeling almost as if she'd just run into a brick wall.

If she hadn't been watching him when the consultant had called for her to assist in beginning the care of the most life-threatening cases she

would never have seen the expression of desolation and loss that crossed his starkly handsome
face. For the first time she had an idea of the
extent of the devastation Gregor would feel if
there *wasn't* anything Rick d'Agostino could do
to get his legs functioning properly again.

That thought hung over her head like a big
black cloud, not in the least bit lifted even when
their first two patients turned out to be relatively
easy to stabilise, thanks to the expert immediate
care by the paramedics on scene.

The patient with the collapsed lung had been
swiftly transferred up to a ward once the tests
had confirmed that there was no uncontrolled
bleeding in the chest cavity. The young man with
the broken legs hadn't been quite so quick to be
transferred up to Theatre, the diagnosis of a fractured pelvis on top of bilateral tibiae and fibulae
causing a delay until everything had been stab-
ilised well enough to ensure that there would be
no catastrophic haemorrhage en route.

'Here we go again,' warned the senior nurse in
charge of managing their resus room as she put
the phone down. 'Mother's insisting on being
with her and she's heading towards hysteria.'

'Keep her out of the way, somebody,' the consultant ordered briskly, and Olivia saw him wince at the wailing that was coming closer by the second. 'Paperwork…*anything* to keep her out of our hair until we know what we're dealing with.'

Olivia could understand a mother being distraught at the thought of her child being injured, but for the moment her sympathies were entirely with the consultant and his team who would need all their concentration to take care of the injured youngster.

'This is Sherilee. She's seventeen,' began the paramedic as the trolley was wheeled swiftly into position. While he continued to make his report, hands all around the immobilised slender figure were transferring the connections of all the mobile monitoring equipment to the hospital system and the resulting cacophony of shrilling beeps was almost deafening for several minutes.

'Please,' Olivia saw her say, the word completely lost behind the mask and the surrounding activity.

Pausing to lean closer, she lifted a hand to warn her colleagues to keep the noise down for a moment.

'What's the matter Sherilee? What did you want to say?' Her heart clenched when she saw the panic in the young woman's wide dark eyes, wondering if it was the same terror that Gregor had felt when he'd first realised that he might be seriously injured.

'What are they talking about?' Her voice, when it emerged, was barely above a whisper. 'What's a *step deformity*? Why am I strapped down? I was wearing a seat belt…honestly, I was.'

'We know you were, sweetheart,' Olivia reassured her, wrapping a gloved hand around the trembling fingers, careful not to dislodge the oxygen perfusion monitor from her finger. 'But some seat belts are more efficient than others, so we're taking all the right precautions to make sure that you don't do yourself any further injury.'

'But—'

'That means we're going to be doing a whole lot of tests and taking pictures and asking questions, and all you have to do is lie there and relax,' she encouraged with a smile.

'I won't be able to relax until someone tells me what a step deformity is,' she insisted, the tremble in her voice doing little to mask her determination.

Olivia smiled. She should have realised that the young woman wasn't going to be put off until she'd had the answers she wanted as soon as she'd seen the stubborn intelligence in those eyes. She'd been seeing something similar ever since the first day she'd met Gregor.

A quick glance up at the consultant gained her a nod to make an explanation, but his pointed glance towards the radiographer told her it wouldn't be long before she had to move aside for the first set of pictures to be taken.

In a sudden blinding flash she remembered that she and Gregor had made love without any thought for the potential new life they might have been creating, so the last thing she needed was to be too close to X-rays.

'Who told you about the step deformity?' she asked, trying to find out just how much she might have overheard.

'One of the rescue guys practically shouted it in my ear when they were getting ready to get me out of the car,' she said with a grimace. 'I'd just told him that I'd been sitting still for so long waiting for them to cut the roof off and get the others out that my legs were feeling all pins-

and-needles. He slid his hand down my back, almost to my waist, and then he shouted, 'Step deformity' and everyone suddenly stood still, as if…as if they were playing a game of statues.'

There were several chuckles at that, and Olivia felt a strange sense of pride that the seventeen-year-old should be able to show such resilience in spite of her fear.

'Well, what he meant was that when the car crashed, the lower half of your body was held still by the lap belt, but the top half wasn't held at all, so it was thrown forward.'

'And?' she prompted shakily, still obviously determined to have her answer.

'And that can stretch—or even tear—the muscles and ligaments that hold the bones of the spine in position, letting them move further forward than they should. So, what we have to do now is a whole load of tests to see how far out of line the bones have moved, and whether they're going to be able to go back on their own or whether we need to do something to help them.'

'But—'

Olivia was loath to interrupt when Sherilee obviously still had more questions to ask, but she was getting the signal that, for the moment, there was no time left for talking.

'I promise we'll talk again when everyone's finished doing their tests. We'll have a better idea of what we need to do to sort you out by then,' she said, giving the slender hand a reassuring squeeze. 'In the meantime, you could have a look at the scenery. There are some quite good-looking blokes around here.'

This time it was Sherilee's turn to give a brief chuckle. 'And if I can't pull a good-looking bloke when I'm lying here in my prettiest under-wear...' she said wryly, then went quite pink when someone in the room gave a wolf-whistle.

'That's quite enough of that!' the consultant said sternly, drawing everyone's attention back to the serious business in hand, but Olivia saw the encouraging wink he gave their young patient as he patted her hand, then stepped back for the radiographer to do her job.

CHAPTER SEVEN

'I AM sorry!' Gregor apologised when his swift, silent progress along the corridor startled an elderly patient into a shriek of shock when she suddenly realised he was beside her. 'Perhaps I should have a warning bell to ring, like a bicycle.'

Or perhaps he should get his bad mood under control so that he noticed that there were other people around him. It wasn't Livvy's fault that she was the obvious person to work beside the consultant, nor that he was becoming increasingly convinced that Rick d'Agostino was going to tell him that there was nothing further he could do for him.

Then there was the way he was letting thoughts of Livvy's almost-wedding and almost-groom get to him, which was ludicrous, especially when he couldn't help but admit that the beautifully

polished wealthy young man was a far better
match for her, socially and financially, to say
nothing of the fact that all the man's body parts
were in working order.

And it wasn't as if he was in a position to come
over all Neanderthal about the situation either.
He couldn't even stand up on his own two feet,
let alone fight for her.

The first person he saw when he reached the
doorway was Livvy, and everything within him
growled 'mine' when he saw the way her slender
body was outlined by the shapeless cotton scrubs
as she leant towards the array of X-rays and
scans displayed on the far wall.

'Livvy?' he called when she straightened and
took a step back, and his heart took an extra beat
at the way she immediately whirled towards the
sound of his voice with a smile on her face. 'I
got a message. Did you need me for something?'

'Yes, please, Gregor.' She made her careful way
around the leads and paraphernalia surrounding
the patient, beckoning him closer. 'I was hoping
you could have a word with Sherilee.'

'Oh, no!' the young woman gasped in a shaken
voice as he came to a halt by her side, his

position in the wheelchair only just bringing him up high enough to make eye contact with her when she was still firmly strapped into immobility on a backboard.

'Excuse me?' He hesitated when he saw the terror in the young woman's eyes. 'Is there something wrong? Can I help you?'

To his surprise, the fear hardened into bitterness in the blink of an eye.

'That's rather unlikely, isn't it?' she pointed out angrily. 'They probably only wheel you in to prepare the patients to be told they're going to end up in a chair, like you...useless for the rest of your life.'

He recognised the choked-off exclamation and knew that Livvy was quite likely to leap to his defence, but in case she or anyone else in the room was thinking of interceding, he put up a single hand to stop them. This definitely wasn't the time to look away from the open challenge in a pair of devastated blue eyes.

'I'm pleased to meet you, too, Sherilee,' he began wryly, but he knew that the only way to stop the young woman's impending hysteria was to confront what she'd just said, head on. 'My name is Gregor and, far from being useless, I'm one of the A and E doctors who've been taking care of your friends.'

For several long seconds, in spite of the fact that there must have been nearly a dozen people in the room, the only sound was the rhythmic click and bleep of the multitude of monitors and sensors.

'Oh, God, I'm *so* sorry!' the young woman wailed, shattering the silence. 'I don't know what…why…'

'Of course you do,' he countered, placing his hand gently over hers so that he didn't disturb the sensor that was monitoring her oxygen perfusion. 'It's because you're scared, and when you're scared, it's perfectly normal to snap and snarl, like a wounded animal.'

'Did you?' she challenged sharply and he was hard-pressed not to grin because, at that moment, she reminded him so much of Livvy.

'I still do,' he admitted. 'Ask anyone here.'

'So you really do work here?' she asked with understandable disbelief. 'But what *can* you do when you're stuck in a wheelchair?'

'Well, I'm getting to be a dab hand with the superglue,' he offered, and someone laughed in the background, but he owed it to the panicking young woman to treat her seriously. 'I've also put in several dozen stitches in your friends, where they were cut up in the accident, and hopefully, once they've healed, you'll hardly see where they were hurt.'

'How are they all?' she demanded, generous-spirited enough to be easily diverted to her friends' plight rather than concentrating on her own.

'Most of them walked away from the crash with little more than aches and pains and a few sutures.' And were extremely lucky to have got away so lightly, if the paramedics were to be believed. 'The passenger behind the driver of the other car had his lung punctured by a broken rib, but that's under control now, and should heal without any problems. The other one—from the front passenger seat in your car—is in Theatre at the moment while they use a big box of expensive screws to put his legs back together.'

'Will Liam walk again?' There was an audible quiver in her voice when she forced the question out.

'It might take him several months of hard graft,' Gregor admitted, 'and he'll probably hate physios for ever by the time he gets there, but there is a very good orthopaedic team here, so you chose the right area to have your prang.'

'If they're so good, how come you're still in *your* chair?' she countered with a sudden return to belligerence.

'Ah. A good question,' he conceded, deliberately stopping himself from looking at Livvy standing quietly beside him. He hoped he'd managed to hide from both of them the spasm of fear that had clenched every muscle in his body at the thought that the news waiting for him in Rick d'Agostino's office would condemn him to this life. 'But I have only come under the care of this hospital very recently. They haven't had time to work their magic on me yet.' And in spite of all the tests he'd undergone, he had no idea if there was any magic left to perform.

'I don't know whether I believe in magic any more,' Sherilee admitted in an uncanny echo of his own thoughts, her voice suddenly sounding so very young. 'If there was magic, someone would be able to wave a wand and I'd be able to get up and walk out of here with just a few bruises. As it is…' Her voice died away unhappily and with the straps holding her to the backboard, she couldn't even do the apparently nonchalant shoulder shrug that was so much a trademark of teenagers these days.

'As it is, young lady, we've taken all our pictures and your mother has finished all the paperwork and will be here in a minute, so we can tell you all the results,' the orthopaedic consultant announced into the lull.

Gregor had to give the man his due. It had only been a matter of hours since his last appointment with Rick d'Agostino, and he'd be seeing him again as soon as this emergency had been dealt with, but the consultant didn't betray the fact by as much as the flicker of an eyelash. Once he'd nodded to Livvy and himself as fellow professionals, his focus had been entirely on their patient and his examination of the results of all the aspects of her tests.

The increased tension in the room while they waited for Sherilee's mother to arrive seemed to affect everyone, but especially the injured youngster, who'd begun to shake visibly.

'Hey,' Gregor murmured softly, leaning

forward to give her hand a squeeze. 'Don't spoil it now. Not with your mother coming in.'

'What do you mean, spoil it?' she said through teeth that were starting to chatter, even though the room was warm enough to make sweat prickle along his spine.

'Well, you've been absolutely brilliant so far,' he said quietly, keeping his words soft enough so that only the three of them could hear him, and he flicked a glance up towards Livvy. 'Isn't that right, Livvy? I think she's held herself together better than most adults.'

'Certainly better than most of the *men* we get in here,' Livvy agreed with a grin that teased a glimpse of one from Sherilee's pale face. 'And the bigger they are, the harder they seem to fall. It's we women who know how to focus on the really important things—like you did when the emergency guys were taking so long to get you out of the car safely. They told us how you kept it all together while they were making all that noise cutting through the glass and metal to take the top off, so they didn't have to waste any time dealing with tears and tantrums.'

'So, if you can hang on just a little bit longer—

until this lot has gone on to the next patient—'
he gestured towards the busy throng surrounding her, every one of them performing some essential task or other '—then, you can have the
longest, noisiest tantrum of your life and none
of them will ever know. They'll still be telling
everyone about this absolutely amazing patient
who never lost her cool.'

'Did you lose yours?' she challenged
suddenly, her eyes suspiciously bright as she
clung to his hand.

'Yes…and no,' he said with a grin to hide the
dark memories of all the nights he still woke
from the nightmares quivering and soaked in
sweat. 'One of the things about the country I
come from is that we have the most amazing-
sounding swear words…and lots of words that
sound as if they should be swear words, even
though they aren't.'

There was a disturbance over by the door and
a red-eyed woman with a large handful of paper
hankies stood there whimpering and gasping for
breath with a horrified expression on her face as
she caught her first sight of her injured daughter
without the paramedic's blanket covering her.

'Promise me something,' Sherilee begged urgently, tugging him closer as her mother started across the room towards her.

'If I can,' Gregor agreed, in spite of the warning frown that Livvy was sending him.

'If I can hold it together through the next ten minutes, promise me you'll teach me some of those swear words?'

'You're not really going to teach her to swear, are you?' Livvy demanded as the two of them paused in the corridor, watching Sherilee disappear into the lift on her way up to the surgical floor.

'I'll have to, after the way she kept her part of the bargain,' Gregor said with a grin, grateful for any conversation that kept Livvy at his side just a little bit longer. They might be temporarily working in the same department but he'd hardly caught more than a fleeting glimpse of her until he'd been surprised by that call from Livvy that she wanted him to come and talk to a patient.

'It's difficult to remember that Sherilee's only seventeen,' Livvy mused as he watched her lean against the nearest wall, pressing her back and shoulders against it to relieve the ache that always came with long spells of bending over a patient. He wondered if she realised that it was a position that thrust her breasts into prominence against the thin cotton of her scrubs top, then had to drag his eyes away before he had to rearrange his own clothing.

The fact that he hadn't had to think about such a problem for longer than he cared to remember wasn't important. It had been a surprise and a delight to discover that those parts were definitely in full working order, but now he needed to concentrate on the other aspects of their relationship. If his meeting with Rick d'Agostino went well, he had every intention of making sure that Livvy had no excuse for wanting to end their marriage…in fact, he was determined that she would want him in her life every bit as much as he needed her in his.

When she glanced at him with a quizzical look he realised that she was waiting for a reply but for a moment he couldn't remember what they'd been talking about. The fact that he was still sat facing the lift into which Sherilee had recently disappeared gave him the clue he needed.

'She definitely isn't your average teenager,' he agreed easily. 'She not only held herself together but managed to stop her mother breaking down completely.'

'How many hours do you think she'll be in Theatre?' she mused, but that was one topic he'd rather not think about it, not with the possibility of similar surgery in his own near future. Sometimes, the fact that he was a doctor was a real disadvantage. At least most of the patients were in happy ignorance of everything that would happen to them and exactly how many things could go wrong while they were under the surgeon's knife.

'Long enough for us to finally get something to eat,' he said firmly, pivoting the chair towards the cafeteria at the other end of the ground floor of the hospital. 'We'll both be in danger of screwing our kidneys up if we don't get some liquid going through our systems.'

'That's part and parcel of working in A and E, I'm afraid,' she grumbled as she kept pace beside him. 'There are always too many patients and too few staff and there's no way we can drink when we're surrounded by who knows what…unlike the office staff, who can have a mug of coffee on their desk and top up at will.'

'But would you rather have their job than your own?' he asked, already knowing the answer because he'd known how dedicated she was to their profession right from the first day he'd met her.

'When is she going to give up?' Livvy demanded, clearly exasperated as she deleted the latest batch of messages from her mother.

'At least that's something you can do remotely,' Gregor pointed out with a grin. 'I wouldn't put it past her to be sitting outside the flat, waiting for us to sneak back in.'

'Please!' Livvy scoffed. 'My *mother* sitting waiting outside the flat? Not likely! It would be some paid minion, bored out of their mind.'

'Well, in that case, I hope they're being *well* paid,' he said, keeping the conversation going rather than letting himself think about what was going to happen in the next few minutes.

So far, he had no idea what arrangements Rick d'Agostino's secretary had made for his stay in the hospital, and the last thing he needed was to find himself on a ward where all the staff knew exactly who he was. When the nightmares came…as they always did, sooner or later…he would far prefer to be anonymous. Otherwise word would be all round the hospital that the doctor in the wheelchair had more than a few screws loose, and that wouldn't do his professional reputation any good at all.

But what option did he have?

The last thing he wanted was to burden Livvy with caring for him in surroundings that hadn't been set up to facilitate the daily care of someone who was essentially paraplegic. She already looked exhausted after a stressful shift in A and E, and he could only guess what sort of toll it was having on her to be aware of everyone's curiosity about her aborted wedding.

She hadn't said anything to him, but, knowing how much she detested being in the limelight, she must be hating the fact that she was surrounded by colleagues who were just dying for her to provide all the juicy details.

On top of that, there was *his* appearance on the scene, and even though Rick d'Agostino's secretary had registered his surname as Davidov, it probably hadn't taken the gossips very long to join up the dots and realise that he was Livvy's husband, especially as there were some who would still remember him from when he'd been training.

'Here we are,' Livvy said brightly as she swung the door open then stopped in consternation, clearly surprised by what she could see.

He craned his neck around the door frame and found himself looking into what must be one of the newly-appointed family rooms that he'd been hearing about today, built so that parents could be close to their sick children.

'You're sure we're supposed to come here?' He paused in the doorway, trying to come to terms with this development. 'I was expecting…well, I'm not really sure *what* I was expecting, as I'm not an in-patient—yet!'

He was intrigued to realise that she looked almost embarrassed. 'I thought Rick d'Agostino was arranging for one of those grotty rooms for single staff for you while I used on-call accommodation. I couldn't understand why he winked when his secretary handed me the key and said he'd decided that this would be the best solution for you, as his patient. Anyway, you should only be taking those elephant-strength painkillers under hospital supervision, so…'

Her words died away and he realised that her eyes were riveted on something across the room and, for the first time, saw that the sofa-bed had been pulled out and made up as a double bed.

This time it was harder to control his response to thoughts of sharing a bed…*that* bed…with the woman standing so uncertainly beside him.

Not that he was in the least bit tempted to give her the option of sleeping elsewhere. If he'd been handed the possibility of spending the night with Livvy at his side, he was going to grab it with both hands and hold on tight. After all, once Rick d'Agostino told him the verdict, it might turn out to have been the last time he slept by her side…ever.

'Thank you, Livvy,' he said quietly, and she frowned.

'For what?'

'I was worried that I was going to have to sleep in a ward, and even if it was a single side room, there's no way that the whole ward wouldn't hear me when the nightmares come. So, thank you for not objecting to sharing a room with me.'

She was silent for several moments and while he could almost hear her thoughts as she processed what he'd just said, he couldn't help feeling guilty for manipulating her like that. Knowing Livvy's soft heart, even if she hadn't liked the fact that his consultant had organised a double room for them, there was no way, now, that she would ask for the arrangements to be changed.

'Unfortunately, the bathroom is only marginally better organised for someone in a wheelchair than our own,' she commented after exploring the en suite. 'But it does have a pull-down seat in the shower.'

That was a shame, he thought, realising that there would be no need for Livvy to accompany him while he took his shower. If he'd been able to claim that he needed her to help, that could have led to…

It was definitely time he turned his thoughts to other topics. The last thing he wanted was for her to feel uncomfortable with him, even though imagining the two of them showering together was a far more pleasurable topic than thinking about his upcoming appointment with Rick d'Agostino.

Unfortunately, it was obvious from her preoccupied air that Livvy had other things on her mind than taking a shower with him and they prepared for bed with hardly a word being spoken, until finally she slid under the covers beside him.

After their earlier love-making, he half expected her to turn to him, the way she always had once they'd started sharing a bed, her head nestling against his shoulder as if that place had been specially constructed just for her.

Instead, there was nearly an arm's length between them and the way tension filled that space told him that she'd made an important decision.

He swallowed hard, wondering if the lump in his throat was his heart trying to beat its way out of his body as he waited for Livvy to speak.

'Tell me why, Gregor,' she demanded, dread a leaden weight inside her as she wondered if she was doing nothing more than hastening the end of their marriage by asking for answers she might not want to hear. 'I need to know why you didn't let me know you were alive as soon as you got your memory back…or, at least, as soon as you returned to England.'

Olivia didn't dare allow herself to look at him, terrified that, for the first time in his life, Gregor might lose that enviable control and reveal what he was *really* thinking, rather than what he was allowed to tell her. Knowing the sort of person he was, she was sure there must have been a good reason; something beyond military rules and regulations; something he could only explain as soon as he was free to do so; something that was just about the two of them—Gregor and Olivia—and the relationship she'd believed was strong enough to survive anything.

She was so busy trying to brace herself for the blow of hearing him say that he hadn't contacted her because her feelings no-longer mattered that it took her a while to realise that he'd been silent far too long.

'Gregor?' Automatically, she turned to look at him and her heart clenched to see the unexpected misery on his face before he tried to conceal it.

Immediately, she castigated herself for being more interested in her own concerns than with his far greater needs. 'What's the matter, Gregor? Are you in pain?' she demanded, reaching out across the expanse of no-man's land stretching between them.

'I'm all right,' he said hoarsely, but she could feel a slight tremor in the strong fingers wrapped around hers. 'Well, as all right as any coward can be,' he added gruffly.

'Coward?' That was a word she would never associate with this man.

'What else would you call it when I deliberately delayed telling you I was alive?'

'Deliberately?' Her brain was so scrambled with incomprehension that she was reduced to parroting words. Was he really telling her that he hadn't wanted her to know that he was alive? That if she hadn't been about to get married, he would never have told her?

'I wanted to wait,' he said.

'Wait? Wait for what?' she demanded hotly. 'I'd already been waiting nearly two years. Don't you think that was long enough to find out that you weren't dead?'

'I didn't think another few weeks would make much difference, not if it meant—'

'Wouldn't make much difference?' Disbelief roared through her. 'Wouldn't make much difference to whom? To you, maybe not, but to me…?'

How could he be so casually callous? As if she hadn't missed him and mourned him for every second since she'd been told that he was lost for ever?

Incensed beyond bearing, she flung the covers back, not knowing where she was intending to go; only intent on being somewhere other than with a man who cared so little for her feelings.

'Livvy, no!' Gregor reached for her arm, holding her just tight enough to prevent her from leaving. 'I didn't mean that the way it sounded.' He reverted to his native language for several heated seconds. 'Please…let me explain. Please…!'

She glared at the hand manacling her wrist but had to admit, when he removed it, that there wasn't even a temporary mark on her skin, despite the potential power in those long fingers and the training he had undoubtedly received when he'd joined the army.

'So, what *did* you mean?' She transferred her glare to that starkly handsome face and the liquid-silver eyes that closed for several telling seconds before he fixed them on her.

'I didn't want to come to you like this,' he said
starkly. 'I wanted to wait long enough to get on
my feet…so I wasn't a cripple any more…so I
wouldn't have to see pity in your eyes.'

'And have you?' she demanded, trying desperately to shore up her anger even though he'd virtually demolished it with one stumbling
sentence. 'Have you seen pity in my eyes, even
for one second?'

One corner of that beautiful mouth kicked up
in a wry half-smile. 'I admit it. Not for one second
have I seen pity,' he agreed. 'I've seen compas-
sion, sympathy, concern…so many emotions.'

He sighed heavily, and the judder in his breath
reminded her that, much as he would hate to
admit it, he wasn't the strong man he'd been
before if their recent, highly charged conversation could shake him so badly. In fact, honesty
compelled her to admit that while she would like
nothing more than to clear the air between them
completely—to find out whether he was willing
to put their marriage back together or had already
decided he wanted a divorce and a fresh start—
what he needed more than anything else tonight
was at least eight hours of nightmare-free sleep.

And if she was left wakeful beside him, savouring the fact that it had been nothing more than male pride that had kept him away from her for one extra day, it was worth it just to have him here now. She'd spent nearly two dreadful years missing him—believing that he was gone for ever and with him her only hope for a family. From now on she was going to relish every moment they were together.

For the second morning in a row, Olivia woke up to find herself wrapped around Gregor as closely as ivy wrapped around a tree...and with absolutely no desire to remove herself.

This was where she wanted to be, every night for the rest of her life.

OK, she'd been hurt and angry that he hadn't let her know he was still alive as soon as he'd regained his memory. But, now that she knew his reason, it didn't really matter why Gregor had delayed a few days before reappearing in her life.

Admittedly, if he'd turned up straight away it would have avoided the fiasco in the church, but what mattered most was that he was back, and regardless of how much or how little Rick d'Agostino could do for his mobility, he was still the only man she would ever love.

When she'd thought she'd lost him for ever, she'd discovered that there had been a gaping hole in her life that only Gregor could fill.

How many times had she lain awake in the night trying desperately to remember the exact smell of his skin just there, in the tender angle between his neck and his shoulder? How many times had she longed for just one more minute of feeling his steady heartbeat under her palm where it spread, here, across the muscular swell of his *pectoralis major*? How many times had her fingertips tingled with the remembered pleasure of stroking these silky dark hairs as they formed such an eye-catching design over his chest and…?

'Woman, you'll drive me insane if you keep doing that,' Gregor growled, the words rumbling around in the broad chest under her ear.

She froze for a second, suddenly realising what she'd been doing, but she couldn't help the happy smile she could feel spreading over her face as she lifted her head to look down at him.

'I'm *so* sorry,' she said penitently, lifting her

hand away from him and leaving it hovering in mid-air. 'I hadn't realised that I was touching you like that. Would you rather I left you alone?'

'What I would *rather* is that you stop teasing me,' he said as he caught her hand and brought it to his mouth for a kiss before pressing it to his chest again in exactly the same place. 'What I would *rather*—' the word emerged almost as a guttural growl, his accent suddenly very obvious '—is that you will make love to me until I can't see straight.'

He drew in a shuddering breath, his dark eyes gazing up into hers full of heartbreaking vulnerability. 'What I would *rather* is that our love-making could make the last two years disappear, but…'

'I'll definitely be happy to try,' she whispered against his lips, wishing there *was* some way to erase all the misery he'd gone through…was still going through. 'But all I can guarantee is to make the next hour or so vanish in…in a haze of ecstasy.'

'A haze of ecstasy?' he repeated with raised eyebrows, then deliberately raised both arms until they bracketed his head on the pillow, leaving himself completely defenceless and at her mercy, then he grinned wickedly at her. 'I like the sound of that, and you can start as soon as you like,' he said.

It didn't take an hour to have both of them breathless and shuddering with the aftershocks of one of the most earth-shattering climaxes they'd ever shared, but there was lingering sadness for Olivia.

It wasn't that they hadn't shrieked each other's names, because they never had done, neither of them able to articulate a single word when the ecstasy between them was that intense. No, it was the memory of her own private guilty pleasure throughout their marriage that, whenever he'd impaled her to the hilt in those seconds when he'd spilled his seed deep inside her, she'd always imagined that this was the time that they would start a new life…a child that would embody all that was best and strongest in both of them as proof of their love.

It had been a crazy, impossible fantasy when they'd agreed that they wouldn't start their family until he'd finished his tours of duty in the more perilous parts of the globe, and they'd been taking precautions to prevent it. Still, each time it had left her with a little glow that one day…one day soon…when Gregor rose over her to drive himself into the deepest reaches of her body, he would leave a permanent tangible memory of their mating that would take his or her place in the world nine months later.

Would that ever happen now?

Her heart gave an extra beat at the thought of the possible consequences of their unprotected love-making yesterday and today, but at this point in her cycle there was little chance that anything would come of it.

And despite the fact that Gregor was the only man she would ever want to be the father of their children, she couldn't avoid the realisation that Rick d'Agostino's verdict could have a profound effect on their plans for a family.

She was unhappy that Gregor seemed to have deliberately arranged his appointment so that she couldn't be present, feeling that this was just one more important part of his life from which she was being excluded, but she could hardly complain, not when she still had such a devastating secret of her own to reveal.

'Ah, Livvy,' he murmured, and even though she shivered deliciously when his fingertips traced the length of her spine and he ended up by cupping her bottom in both hands, she wondered whether this might be the right time to tell him, while they were sated and relaxed and...

No. Not today, she decided, not absolutely certain whether it was cowardice that made the choice, or consideration for the fact that he had enough on his mind with his upcoming appointment.

Well, she was going to have to tell him some time soon. If they were to have a chance of making their marriage work, there would have to be honesty between them, after all, there was no point pretending that she wanted anyone else in her life. She loved Gregor more than she'd ever loved anyone else in the world and that wasn't going to change, no matter what verdict Rick d'Agostino gave him.

'So, what you're saying is that you're confident that, if you operate, you'll be able to get me back up on my feet?' Gregor recapped to give his whirling thoughts a few extra seconds to process the information.

If he went under Rick d'Agostino's knife, it would be a matter of weeks—well, months, if he was being more realistic—but he would finally be out of this hateful chair for ever... Well, at least until old age finally took its toll.

'Obviously, there are no guarantees,' the orthopaedic surgeon cautioned.

'There never are,' Gregor agreed wryly.

'But all the tests confirm that there is no basic neurological reason why you can't walk. It's purely the fact that there was mis-union and non-union after your initial surgeries...for whatever reason...and this has resulted in the fact that your pelvis and legs are non-weight-bearing.' He pointed again to several images among the array of X-rays lined up along the bank of light boxes. 'We'll need to do some fairly heavy-duty bone-grafting here...and here...for which we'll probably need to use donated or cadaveric bone. Do you have any objections to the use of donated bone matter?'

'None whatever, if it can get me on my feet again,' Gregor said, marvelling that some people were generous enough to donate their bodies for the use of others after their deaths. With the advent of the use of donated skin, bone, tendons and ligaments, the number of people whose lives could be improved by just one person's foresight could now be counted in dozens rather than the two or three when it was only possible for hearts and kidneys to be transplanted.

'Now we come to the other side of the "advised consent" equation,' d'Agostino warned. 'There are, of course, the usual possibilities for problems to occur during surgery, including unexpected allergic reactions to drugs used during the anaesthetic leading to anaphylactic shock or even cardiac arrest.'

Gregor waved a dismissive hand. As far as he was concerned, a doctor was only too well aware of the myriad variables that could go wrong, so this part of the speech was just a waste of both their time, although the hospital's ethics committee would no doubt disagree.

'Then there are the potential side-effects if the surgery doesn't go as well as we expect.' The serious expression on the man's face made his heart give an extra thump.

'Side-effects *other* than the fact I could go through all of it and still end up in this chair?' Suddenly he had an awful feeling where this conversation was going.

'Unfortunately, until we get in there, we won't be able to see how much scar-tissue was left—both by the initial injury, then by the surgeries—so, at this point, in spite of all the scans, X-rays and MRIs, some of our plans are pure guess-work,' he admitted. 'But one of the dangers is that we'll need to deal with the area through which the nerves leading to your genital area travel, and unfortunately there's a chance that...'

He hardly needed to complete *that* sentence. Gregor understood only too well what permanent damage to that bundle of nerves could do to him. In fact, he'd spent nearly two years believing that it had already happened, until he'd seen Livvy again and his body's natural reaction had proved otherwise.

At that point, and especially the last two mornings, when Livvy had demolished two years of longing with her generous love-making, he'd believed *that* worry had been banished for ever, but that obviously wasn't the case.

'You're saying that the operation could leave me permanently impotent. That there's a chance that I'd never be able to make love again,' Gregor said for him, feeling as sick as if he'd taken a body-blow.

Somewhere, there must be some cosmic laughter going on.

As he'd told her last night, when he'd regained his memory he'd been determined not to contact Livvy until he could meet her on his own two feet. Her imminent marriage had scuppered that plan, forcing him to go to her as a wreck of the man he'd once been.

Now, when the probability of walking again was almost within his grasp, he was hit with the possibility of having that which was most male about him rendered useless. And after the mind-blowing love-making he'd shared with Livvy just hours ago, that was an irony beyond belief.

How was he supposed to make that sort of choice?

He certainly didn't want to remain in the wheel-chair for ever…for one thing, statistics showed that it would significantly shorten his life, to say nothing of the fact that it would limit his career prospects and probably prevent him from earning a good enough living to support a family.

Then there was the fact that he wanted Livvy to be his wife and the mother of the children they both wanted, not reduced to the permanent role of carer while also taking on the burden of being the primary wage-earner for the two of them.

And if he *did* have the operation and the worst happened, leaving him impotent, how long would Livvy stay with him if he was never going to be able to satisfy her? How would he cope, his male ego reduced to nothing when the only way he would be able to give her the family they'd planned was by resorting to mechanical means?

Livvy deserved a *whole* man…one who could support her and satisfy her both in and out of the bedroom. If the worst-case scenario happened, it looked as if he was going to be left with an either/or choice, and that wasn't good enough—not for his Livvy.

'So, what do you say?' Rick d'Agostino closed the file on his desk and spread both hands over the cover as he met Gregor's eyes straight on. 'I can put you in the schedule as early as Monday, using one of my allocated theatre slots. Shall I book it?'

'Monday?' Something that felt very like panic roared through him. He had to make a decision about Monday *now*? It didn't feel as if he would be ready to decide a *year* from Monday. 'Ah, can I get back to you about that?' he said, certain it sounded as if he was gabbling in his haste to leave the room. His hands were already manoeuvring the chair away from the desk, swivelling to point it towards the door.

'Of course you can,' the consultant agreed. 'Obviously you need to have a word with your wife and tell her what's going on. I'll hear from you later, then.'

The final words followed Gregor out of the door as he headed as fast as he could towards the nearest bathroom, desperate to get there before he lost his breakfast and disgraced himself.

CHAPTER EIGHT

'I THOUGHT the words Olivia and workaholic had been permanently welded together. It's good to see that they haven't,' said a voice from the doorway, and Olivia nearly tipped her cup over herself.

Unfortunately, the man coming across the staffroom wasn't the man she wanted to see.

'Ri—Mr d'Agostino,' she stammered as she tried to fight her way out of a chair that seemed loath to release her from its saggy refuge.

'Rick, please,' he corrected firmly and held a staying hand up. 'Don't get up when you've managed to get the most comfortable seat in the room. The upholstery in most of them is too hard for any sort of relaxation.'

'Perhaps the hospital wants to make sure we don't fall asleep during our tea breaks,' Olivia suggested, marvelling that she was able to put any sort of coherent sentence together while all she could think about was that there must be a major problem with his findings if Gregor's consultant was seeking her out like this.

That fear only intensified when, without even pausing to get himself a drink, the handsome man folded his lean body into the chair beside her.

'So, what's the decision? Is it on for Monday?' he asked, seeming almost boyishly eager as he smiled at her.

'Monday?' Olivia blinked. 'What's happening on Monday? What decision?' Suddenly she realised just how foolish she was being. What else would the orthopaedic surgeon be talking about but…? 'You can operate? You're going to operate on Gregor? You can help him?'

Her overwhelming delight that something could be done for the man she loved almost outweighed the fact that he hadn't come to tell her himself. Then she saw the chagrined expression on the consultant's face and was angry that Gregor's thoughtlessness had caused this embarrassment, especially for a man who seemed so keen to help.

'I'm sorry. I appear to have jumped the gun,'

he apologised. 'I take it Gregor hasn't had a chance to speak to you yet.'

'Or hasn't tried to,' she muttered under her breath, confusion filling her head. If Rick d'Agostino had told Gregor that there was an operation that could help him, why on earth hadn't he come straight to her to let her know the good news…unless…?

'Will the operation give him the chance to get out of the wheelchair—to be able to use his legs again—or was it only going to be able to give him a better quality of life? Or…or did you find other, unexpected problems that—?'

'I'm sorry, Olivia,' he interrupted with a pained expression. 'If Gregor hasn't told you what's going on, then patient confidentiality prevents me from discussing anything with you without his permission.'

'But—'

'I'm really sorry,' he apologised as he unfolded to his full height. 'Just…just ask him to contact me before the weekend if he decides he wants the slot on Monday. Tell him I'll keep it open for him until then.'

Olivia watched, wide-eyed, as the man hurried out of the room and her blood began to boil.

Not that she was angry with Rick. The poor man had been put in that uncomfortable position through no fault of his own. After all, what patient *wouldn't* have hurried back to his nearest and dearest with the news that such an eminent surgeon was willing to operate on him? What normal person wouldn't have been eager to pass on the good news that…?

But that was the problem, wasn't it?

She didn't even know if it *was* good news.

She had no idea whether the orthopaedic surgeon had reached the verdict that he would be able to completely restore Gregor's ability to walk and carry on a normal life, or if he would only be able to relieve some of the pain that still left him intermittently dependent on heavy-duty analgesia nearly two years after he had been injured.

In all probability, the reality would be somewhere between those two extremes, but the very fact that Gregor hadn't come to tell her about it was ominous.

She flicked a glance at the big clock up above the unit housing the tea and coffee and a vast collection of mismatched cups and mugs, and calculated that she had at least another ten minutes before she had to rejoin the fray…longer if the current lull continued until the usual rash of admissions around the time the children came out of school.

Well, that was long enough to track the wretched man down, she decided as she hurriedly rinsed out her cup and tipped it up on the draining board. And the first place she was going to look for that particular wounded animal was in his temporary lair.

She stuck her head round the door of the treatment room he'd made his own over the last couple of days, but it was empty, everything pristinely ready for the next patient who needed it. So, the next stop was the room they'd been allocated, and all the time she was waiting for the lift to arrive, then travelling up in a compartment that seemed to need stop at every single floor on the way, she forced herself to replay in her mind every one of the articles she'd pulled up on the medical website that had anything to do with injuries to the hips, pelvis and lower spine.

By the time she flung open the door to their temporary home, she'd drawn up a comprehensive mental list of all the possible orthopaedic complications that could have been thrown up by the tests Rick would have ordered. She was ready to grill Gregor to find out exactly what problems they would be facing and had even drawn breath to fire the first question at him, but the room was empty.

The bathroom door was open, too, so she didn't even have to set foot over the threshold to know he wasn't there.

She knew he *had* been there, and fairly recently, too. The room was still redolent of the mixture of soap, shampoo and man that lingered in the air from his shower that morning, and she could almost see him, with droplets of water scattered over those impressive shoulders and his dark hair sexily rumpled from his usual haphazard rub with a towel.

Now, she could see that his infamous leather jacket was missing from the back of the chair, but where he would have gone with the threat of rain in the air had her totally stumped.

If he wasn't here and he hadn't offered his services down in A and E after his appointment, where on earth was he? Where could he have gone to lick his wounds…presuming that Rick's conclusions had left him with wounds to lick. Where would *she* choose to go if…?

A mental image of the soothing oasis that they had made of their flat and how much she'd valued it in the dreadful days after she'd been told he was dead told her exactly where Gregor would have gone if he needed time to think.

The fact that he'd needed to do that thinking without her—without even talking to her before he'd left—hurt more than she could have anticipated. Only a few hours ago they'd been as close as any two people could be, physically and mentally…at least, that's what she'd believed.

She'd actually found herself smiling in those few minutes when she'd been able to forget about his appointment with the orthopaedic surgeon, and was certain that at times the smile must have widened into a soppy grin as she'd painted new versions of happily-ever-after inside her head and her heart.

So, what was she going to do about this?

Was she going to nurse her hurt at being shut out, and let it fester?

Was she going to allow his need for some private

time to come to terms with…with whatever Rick had told him…come between them?

Or was she going to grasp the nettle and fight for what she wanted—Gregor in her life, for *all* of her life?

It didn't take long to let A and E know that she needed some personal time, and bearing in mind that she'd been conscripted to fill in for injured colleagues at a moment's notice, Tricia promised to sort matters out for her, with the proviso that she got to hear the whole story at some stage.

'You still owe me the skinny on the wedding-that-never-was,' she reminded Olivia darkly. '*And* for the fact that I warned the rest of them not to bug you until you were ready to talk.'

Even in a taxi, the journey took longer than she expected. Well, she didn't usually do this journey at a time when all the children were coming out of school and the roads were clogged with mothers driving oversized off-roaders as if they were Centurion tanks.

In an effort to take her mind off the possibility that there would be some sort of showdown when she got home, Olivia forced herself to switch her phone on and worked her way through the more important messages that had been accumulating ever since the spectacular cancellation of the wedding.

At least the more earthy goings-on between several members of a reality TV show meant that there were no longer any messages from the press, so the only ones she had to ignore were the dozen or so from her mother, in the hope that she might eventually come to believe the fiction that her daughter had gone away.

'Fat chance!' she muttered under her breath, knowing that her parent's interrogation techniques would eventually give her the information she needed as to Gregor's and her whereabouts. All she could hope was that it would take a little longer—long enough for the two of them to work out what *they* wanted to do with their lives and their marriage—before her mother tried to stick her oar in.

Nerves forced her to take the stairs when she reached their building. She was far too worked-up to want to stand waiting for the elderly lift to arrive. Unfortunately, it meant that she opened the door and burst into the flat panting as if she'd just completed a marathon.

'Livvy!' Gregor exclaimed as he twisted to face the unexpected intruder. 'What on earth is the matter? What is wrong? Why are you here?'

'That's funny. Those were exactly the questions I wanted to ask you,' she said as she deposited her purse and mobile phone on the little table and conscientiously hung her keys on the hook above.

She turned to face him, this time making sure that he was more than a silhouette against the late afternoon sunlight so that she could see his expression.

'Gregor,' she began, but when she caught her first proper look at him and saw just how drained and miserable he looked, somehow she didn't feel like haranguing him any more.

'Oh, Gregor,' she said as she sank onto the nearest chair, her heart heavy inside her. 'I was waiting for you to come and tell me Rick d'Agostino's verdict, and when you didn't come I just told myself that his clinic might be running late. Then I saw him while I was having a tea break and I knew your appointment was over, and then he asked if you'd made your decision about Monday—'

'What else did he say?' he interrupted fiercely. 'What did he tell you?'

'Nothing, of course,' she snapped, instantly imagining the worst if this was the irrational way he was behaving. 'He apologised, politely, but said he couldn't break patient confidentiality.'

Gregor subsided, but he was looking greyer than ever, and her heart ached for everything he was going through. Had the news been that bad that he couldn't face talking about it?

Perhaps it was time to do something completely ordinary, to relieve a little of the pressure.

'Shall I make us a drink, or something to eat?' she suggested, even as she ached to know what he was thinking...share whatever was making him look so depressed.

'That would be good, but I need the bathroom, first,' he said as he grimly wheeled himself across the polished wood floor.

Olivia was listening out for Gregor to exit the bathroom while she loaded the scratch meal on a tray so when her phone rang, she automatically picked it up without thinking what she was doing.

'About time, too, Olivia,' her mother declared

stridently. 'I don't know what you were thinking of, cutting yourself off like that when there are so many things to organise.'

'Hello to you, too, Mother,' she said wryly, but she may as well have saved her breath because the human steam-roller on the other end of the line wasn't taking any notice.

'I've spoken to that friend of your father's who's a QC and he says it's important that the two of you aren't cohabiting. The fact that he isn't dead means that you need to start all over again to apply for a divorce before you can marry the Grayson-Smythe boy, but you can easily get it on the grounds of desertion. It's a good job you'd taken leave from work to go on your honeymoon because that gives you plenty of time to get this mess properly sorted out, once and for all. I've made an appointment for you to speak to him—the QC, that is—tomorrow morning at ten-thirty. He's going to have all the paperwork drawn up and ready for your signature.'

'Mother, I've already spoken to a solicitor—' she tried to tell her, remembering that was one of the calls she'd returned in the taxi just a few minutes ago.

'Oh, good!' she butted-in enthusiastically. 'I presume he contacted you as soon as I instructed him. Did he tell you he'd got everything organised?'

'Mother, I've spoken to my *own* solicitor, to ask him to find out about Gregor's—'

'Stupid girl!' she interrupted. 'Why on earth did you want to waste time doing that? Phone him back and cancel the appointment. You don't need to bother with some tuppenny-ha'penny jumped-up clerk when you can have the services of a top-notch QC. That way it will get done properly so we can get started on rescheduling the wedding. I've already spoken to the vicar…the church seems to get so booked up that I thought I ought to see when was the soonest he had available.'

She barely drew breath before she was off again. 'In fact, tell me the name of the person you spoke to, Olivia, and I'll let him know we've got someone else dealing with it. We want to make sure it's done properly, this time, so that—'

'*No*, Mother,' Olivia interrupted firmly, almost feeling as if she would have to shout to make sure her mother listened.

'Really, Olivia!' she exclaimed in her most disapproving voice. 'There's no need to bellow like that. So uncouth. Now, Ashley is a completely different matter and the sooner we can re-schedule the wedding—'

'This is a totally pointless conversation because I never loved him anyway. It's a recipe for divorce.'

'Rubbish! It's just as easy to love a rich man as a poor one…easier, in fact, especially if he's in line to inherit a title and an estate. And all you have to do is sign the papers to let the QC sort out the divorce and you can have it all. Your father and I can keep an eye on things to make sure he doesn't drag his heels.'

'That's exactly why I *won't* be using your QC. The last thing I want is someone you can browbeat into breaking client confidentiality so you can push things along. Anyway, it's a moot point because I've already instructed my own so-licitor.'

'I expect he's using the fact he's in a wheel-chair to play with your emotions. Is he expect-ing you to use our money to pay for his treatment…or does he even need the thing?'

'Yes, Mother, he definitely does need the wheelchair and, in spite of it, he's already working at the hospital. And the fact that he's on staff means that he has access to any specialist he needs.'

'Well, thank goodness for small mercies!' her mother exclaimed. 'That means you don't need to be tied to him for him to get decent treatment, so you can go ahead with getting the divorce and I can get on with re-booking the wedding.'

'Forget it, Mother,' Olivia snapped, totally out of patience with the woman's one-track mind. 'It isn't going to happen, so don't waste your time. Now, if you don't mind, I've got more important things to do so I'm ending this conversation. Goodbye.'

Her ear was ringing from the verbal onslaught and her head was so full of turbulent thoughts that she almost missed the sound of the wheelchair tyres on the polished floorboards as Gregor came into the room.

'That was a mistake,' she said, rubbing her ear theatrically. 'I completely forgot who might be phoning when I answered it.'

Gregor didn't return her smile, his expressive mouth flattened into an unexpectedly grim line. For the first time in a long time she saw a look of flint in his grey eyes, hard enough to strike sparks, and she wondered just how devastating the surgeon's verdict had been.

Part of her knew that the man she'd married… the man she'd come to know almost as well as she knew herself…needed time to process things inside his head before he was ready to talk about them. She'd also had to learn to accept that *some* things would *never* be discussed.

But this was different.

This didn't just affect Gregor's life. If they were going to remain a married couple—as she fervently hoped they were—then it would affect her, too.

'Gregor, can we talk about it?' she asked when they were settled in the familiar comfort of the sitting room, hating how tentative she sounded. But that was the way her voice came out when everything inside her was tied up in knots.

'Talk about what?' He swung to face her and the expression in his eyes felt like being slashed by jagged-edged blades. 'Is there something you want to tell me, Livvy?'

* * *

Gregor saw the way those beautiful eyes of hers widened at his challenge and the spark of satisfaction that he'd surprised her almost banished the sick despair that had filled him as he'd overheard her conversation with her mother.

He hadn't intended listening…had even tried to block his ears to what was being said…but it had been impossible, especially once he'd heard his own name.

He'd known from the first moment that he'd met Livvy's mother that the woman couldn't stand him because he hadn't been *her* choice of husband for her daughter, but by that stage he and Livvy had been crazily in love and nothing the woman had tried to throw at them had stopped them getting married.

Of course, he'd recognised that he would never be good enough for the only child of the Mannington-Forbes dynasty—for someone as special as Livvy—and he'd thanked his lucky stars that she'd apparently fallen every bit as hard for him as he had for her.

When he'd realised who was on the phone just now, he'd selfishly hoped that he would hear Livvy make some sort of declaration to let her mother know, once-and-for-all, that she was going to stand by him, no matter what the outcome of his surgery.

Instead, in almost the same breath as she'd told her mother that she'd already instructed a solicitor, he'd heard her say that she didn't love him and had spoken about divorce.

And that was before he'd found the guts to tell her that he was having to weigh up the choice between being able to regain the use of his legs against the possibility of losing the use of his manhood.

The longer he held her gaze the more uncomfortable she appeared to become, a look that seemed very like guilt filling her eyes until, finally, she looked away.

An icy shiver snaked its way up his spine, setting every hair on end, and he froze.

The last time he'd felt that sensation had been…had been…

Frantically, he searched his memory, desperate to uncover what felt like vital information.

Suddenly, it burst into lurid detail and he almost groaned aloud as it buried him under an avalanche of impressions…the unforgettable smell of cordite mixed with the rich scent of the earth thrown up by the explosion…the intermittent sharp crack of gunfire making him flinch, each report growing closer and closer as he tried to squeeze just one more of the wounded into the inadequate transport available…trying to ignore the vulnerable feeling of having no bulletproof clothing to protect himself, the multicoloured trousers and jacket he'd thrown on over his blood-spattered operating scrubs nothing more than camouflage-patterned heavy-duty cotton fabric.

He'd felt the presence of danger all around him in those moments when he'd left the dubious safety of a building erected in less vicious times. Perhaps this vividly remembered sensation had been a presentiment of what was going to happen when he'd answered the old man's plea for help for his trapped pupils?

But surely he couldn't be sensing that sort of danger here, in the home he'd shared with the woman who would be a part of every fibre of his being until the end of his days and beyond? There were no hidden snipers or out-of-date boilers ready to explode, just a sensation…an impression that…that there was something coming…something that was going to hurt… something that was going to be even more agonising than waking up to find that not only had he lost the use of his legs but he'd also lost his memory…

Well, he had his memory back, but very little else, and somehow, before tomorrow morning when he had to give his decision to Rick d'Agostino, he had to find the words to tell Livvy just how precarious his situation could be.

It was agonising trying to choose between the real chance that the operation would give him back the use of his legs and the equally real chance that he would never again be able to make love to her.

There wasn't really a choice to be made when he contemplated the possibility of spending the rest of his life in a wheelchair, dependent on others. In comparison with getting his health and strength back—getting his life back— becoming impotent might seem a small sacrifice. But would that leave him with the agony of trying to decide what sort of a future he would have when Livvy finally told him that she didn't want him in her life any more?

The phone shrilled a summons and they both jumped then stared at the instrument waiting for the machine to answer it.

He was almost certain that it would be Livvy's mother again. The woman was noted for her persistence and it didn't sound as if she'd been satisfied with her daughter's response to whatever demands she'd been making.

Instead, it was a male voice, and all his possessive instincts raised their heads and snarled.

'This is Gareth Lloyd from Solomon and Associates with a message for Mrs Olivia Davidson,' the voice said crisply. 'I have completed my enquiries and now have the definitive information she requested concerning—'

Livvy snatched the receiver up, silencing the recording as she broke in. 'Hello, Mr Lloyd, this is Olivia Davidson. Thank you for getting back to me so quickly.' She turned her back on him and Gregor was left fuming as the rest of the call deteriorated into little more than a series of non-committal murmurs.

This time, even though he was openly eavesdropping, he was unable to glean a single thing from the call, other than the fact that the man's precise way of speaking had left him with the impression that he was a lawyer of some sort.

Suddenly, he was convinced that Livvy would take advantage of the fact that they were within the privacy of their own home to break the bad news—that she had taken steps to end their marriage properly this time by filing for divorce—and in spite of the numerous dangers he'd had to face in his life, cowardice clenched a tight hand around his heart and he burst into hasty speech as soon as the call ended.

'Are you ready to go back to the hospital or are you thinking of staying here for the night?' Even as he asked the question his emotions were in such turmoil that he wasn't sure which answer he wanted.

'After speaking to my mother and letting her know I'm at the flat, the chances are that she'll turn up here,' she pointed out with a grimace.

'You don't think she'll have some more important "do" lined up for this evening?' he suggested, ashamed to sound so petty.

'I suppose it's possible,' she conceded calmly. 'She was expecting to be basking in the glorious aftermath of the wedding, this week, and would have accepted all sorts of invitations so that people could tell her how wonderful it had all been and how brilliantly she'd organised the whole thing, so she'll either be keeping her head down until someone in their circle does something more gossip-worthy, or she could have decided to brazen it out...doubtless, blaming the whole fiasco on her dreadful wayward daughter—'

'Or on me for having the bad manners not to die when I was supposed to,' he interrupted wryly. That startled a chuckle out of her that lifted his spirits enough that he decided to risk making a suggestion. 'How about ordering a meal from that little Italian restaurant just off the high street before we go back to the hospital? You know the one I mean...where they make that fabulous marinara...and the home-made pannacotta to the grandmother's own recipe? I think I was fantasising about their food when I was eating yet another bowl of potato soup. Are they still there? Do they still deliver?'

'They're still there,' she confirmed, then hesitated briefly before continuing, 'but I don't know if they still deliver because I haven't had anything from them since…for two years,' she finished quietly.

His eyes burned with the realisation that she must have been avoiding the place ever since he'd disappeared. Had she missed him so much that she hadn't been able to face eating food from their favourite restaurant? The mere possibility was enough to rekindle a spark of hope.

'So, are you going to phone or shall I?' he asked, hoping the huskiness to his voice wasn't as obvious to her as it was to him.

The meal was probably as wonderful as ever, but Olivia found it hard to remember a single mouthful with guilt weighing her down so badly.

It had been bad enough when she had only been hiding one secret—a devastating secret that had been gnawing away at her soul for nearly two years already—but since that phone call from Gareth Lloyd she could almost hear Gregor's mind working as he tried to unravel whatever he'd managed to glean from her deliberately cryptic conversation.

She knew she should tell him. He deserved to know…everything. But there was a small stubborn part of her that kept arguing that *he* was keeping secrets from *her*, too…such as the results of all those tests and the verdict on what sort of recovery Gregor could anticipate.

So, here they were, Olivia thought in frustration, the two of them sitting at either side of the table in silence, each apparently wrapped up in their own thoughts.

She had no idea what was going through Gregor's head…nothing pleasant if the grim expression on his face was anything to go by. And all the while she was struggling to find a way to break the silence with an innocuous topic in the hope that it would lead to the conversation that needed to be broached.

Olivia had just about nerved herself to jump in with both feet when he beat her to the punch.

'When were you intending telling me that you're already going ahead with the divorce?' he demanded, and completely robbed her of the power to speak.

CHAPTER NINE

OLIVIA felt her eyes grow wider and wider as she tried to work out where Gregor could have got such a crazy idea.

'Don't look so surprised,' he growled. 'It was a bit difficult *not* to hear what you were saying when you were discussing it with your mother.'

'With my *mother*?' It took her a moment to switch gears. She'd thought he was referring to her recent conversation with Gareth Lloyd, not the previous one with her mother.

She could remember arguing about the fact that she wouldn't meekly allow herself to be dragooned into using her parents' tame QC, but Gregor couldn't have heard her say she was applying for a divorce because it wasn't true. That was the last thing she wanted to do when she was still so much in love with the man.

'Come on, Livvy! Don't pretend you don't know what you said… "I never loved him. It was a recipe for divorce"… I heard you say it,' he ground out, and if it hadn't been for the pain so clear in his eyes she could have laughed at such a crazy misunderstanding.

'No, Gregor, *no!*' she exclaimed as she speared frustrated fingers through her hair. She was further than ever from bringing up the topic she wanted to discuss, but this definitely needed straightening out first. 'I wasn't talking about *you.*'

'How many men *are* you intending divorcing?' he scoffed as he folded his arms tightly across his chest in a giveaway defensive gesture.

'*None!*' she declared fiercely, then continued quickly before he had a chance to interrupt. '*That's* what the telephone call from Gareth Lloyd was about. I'd asked him to check up on the legal position of our marriage, bearing in mind the fact that you'd been declared dead erroneously.'

'Well, you had to do that to make sure the way was legally clear for you to finally marry the Honourable Double-Barrelled,' he pointed out snidely.

'That would be true if I were in the least bit interested in marrying him,' she countered swiftly. 'If he was *my* choice of husband, I could have married him at any time from when I was sixteen and my mother would have turned cartwheels of joy the length of the Grayson-Smythes' ballroom.'

'But, you *were* about to marry him,' he said impatiently. 'In fact, if I hadn't turned up when I did, you'd be Mrs Double-Barrelled by now— or would that be Countess Double-Barrelled?— and probably well on your way to delighting both families by producing the first of a large brood of junior Double-Barrels.'

'Hardly, because it was never going to be a real marriage,' she blurted out, and it was only when she saw his dark eyebrows shoot up towards his hairline that she realised exactly what she'd said.

'Why on earth not?' he demanded, clearly startled, and she had to admit that it was the obvious question. 'Why else would the offspring of two such well-connected families be marrying if not to produce the next generation…unless the two of you had finally and very conveniently fallen madly in love?'

There was a dark edge to the final question that completely overshadowed the heavy-handed irony that had preceded it, and the expression in Gregor's eyes made Olivia feel more guilty than ever for having given in to her mother's incessant nagging.

It had never felt right to agree to the solemnity of a church wedding when neither she nor Ash was in love. The whole thing had been a travesty from start to ignominious finish, with not a single one of the emotions that had filled her on the day that she and Gregor had made their vows.

Was this her punishment? To have Gregor distrust her so much that he could believe that she would instigate divorce proceedings without even discussing it with him?

'You said you wanted children…or was that a lie?' The question sounded almost like an accusation. 'Was being a doctor always going to be more important to you because you'd had to fight so hard to get there?'

'Not at all,' she said stiffly, feeling as if she was bleeding inside from the wounds he was inflicting, and they were always going to hurt more because of the guilt attached to them. 'But if I tell you…you must promise that you will never tell anyone else. It could destroy Ash, and he doesn't deserve that.'

There was a flash of something hot and angry in his eyes but he blinked and it was gone by the time he shrugged and said, 'Who would I tell?'

'OK, then… I'm not proud of it, but neither Ash nor I wanted a marriage—to each other or anyone else—but because of our families, we were never going to be given any peace until we found a partner so we could "do our duty" by perpetuating the family names.' She paused, distracted by the fierce expression still darkening his face, then forced herself to continue. 'We were hoping that the fact that we never managed to produce a baby for them would be seen as just bad luck and a real tragedy for both dynasties.

'And the truth?' he prompted.

'The truth was that we had no intention of ever sharing a bed, let alone trying to have a baby.'

'Why not?' He shook his head. 'Why would he bother marrying you if he had no intention of…of…?'

'Because it would have broken his partner's heart,' she said simply. 'The two of them have been together for years and Ash would dearly love to formalise their relationship with a civil ceremony, now that single-sex partnerships can be made legal, but he knows he could never do that to his parents.'

She saw the moment when the penny dropped; saw the mixture of comprehension and…was that relief in his expression? Had he honestly thought that she would so easily have been able to forget her love for him; that she could have replaced him in her heart and in her bed?

'Ash is a friend,' she said simply. 'We've known each other, as neighbours, for most of our lives, even though I was never interested in joining the circles he moves in.' There was an acceptance in the way he was looking at her that prompted her to explain further. 'It was because we both knew what was at stake, and how awful it could be if either one of us let the cat out of the bag, that we could even contemplate entering into such an arrangement. It was going to let both of us off the hook so we could get on with our lives without constant family pressure.'

'I can understand wanting to get away from that, and I can see what *he* was getting from the arrangement—a wife in name only who already knew about his boyfriend and accepted the situation—but what were *you* going to get out of it? You could have chosen to marry someone who could give you the children you wanted. Why decide to be childless?'

'Because I wanted *your* child!' she exclaimed, and as her heart clenched inside her with the enormity of the pain she'd been carrying around for nearly two years, she burst into tears.

An hour later, in the taxi taking them back to the hospital, Olivia was still kicking herself for missing out on the most perfect opportunity she was likely to get.

It had been all very well to blurt out that she hadn't wanted any babies if they couldn't be his, and Gregor had been unbelievably tender as he'd brushed away her tears with gentle fingertips, but somehow, even then... Maybe it had been *especially* then—when he had been so overwhelmingly the man she'd first fallen in love with—that she couldn't bear to destroy the moment between them...

There was certainly no chance to bring up an

emotional topic during the taxi ride back to their room in the hospital, and the atmosphere in the enclosed space made her afraid that Gregor was drawing away from her again; putting up an impenetrable barrier between the two of them.

Had he misunderstood what she'd been telling him about the status of their marriage, she wondered, or did he think that, as a result of her mother's legal manoeuvring, their marriage had already been ended? Was he relieved? In which case it would be ironic that his survival meant that their marriage had survived, too. If he did want a divorce, he would have to start back at the beginning of the whole process.

Olivia swallowed hard, everything in her clenched against the very idea before a sudden surge of determination had her squaring her shoulders and raising her chin.

She and Gregor had been lucky to find each other and recognise their perfect other half and their marriage had been good and strong before he'd disappeared. She couldn't believe that even two years without a memory, forced to live as someone else, could have changed the essence of the man she'd loved and who'd loved her in return.

Their marriage was worth fighting for, and once they were ready for bed and she had him at her mercy, she was going to fire the first salvo in her battle to rebuild what they'd so nearly lost. And if that included fighting dirty by donning her sexiest silk nightdress and anointing her pulse points with his favourite perfume before she seduced him into a receptive frame of mind, then so be it.

It was only when they were both back in their borrowed room that Olivia remembered that she'd had a few questions she wanted to ask Gregor before she'd been sidetracked by the need to explain how she'd come to be marrying Ash.

Her heart ached with the realisation that what should have been an impossibly joyful reunion had quickly been marred by anger and resentment on both sides, but with each little revelation…deliberate or otherwise…the animosity had been melting away.

But if the anger was largely gone, the same couldn't be said for the questions that still needed answers, and she was going to make sure she got them, one way or another.

'Gregor,' she began, her heart in her throat, dreading the possibility that she was going to learn that there was very little more that Rick d'Agostino could do for him but anxious that he might be missing out on a better quality of life simply because he couldn't bear the thought of going through the trauma of yet more surgery, 'why *didn't* you take up the offer of the surgical slot straight away? I know Rick's willing to operate, so I don't understand why you're hesitating. Did he tell you some-thing…about your current situation, or the prognosis after the operation…that put you off? Did he shoot down the idea that he could get you on your feet after all?'

It was a good job she wasn't holding her breath as she waited for an answer because the silence seemed to stretch on for ever.

'*Please*, Gregor. Talk to me!' she begged, tears still horribly close to the surface. 'All I know is that you've had an enormous number of tests and have been offered surgery. I need to know more. I need to know what he found. Did he say the damage you suffered makes it hopeless? Or perhaps it was the other surgeons' attempts that caused the problems? Would this operation just be aimed at stabilising things to reduce your pain?'

'Not at all,' he said in a strangely grim tone. 'He seems pretty confident that the operation will finally get me out of this thing.' He slapped both hands on the arms of the chair for emphasis, but she could tell that there was something else on his mind...something that he wasn't telling her.

So, if it was something that he couldn't tell her openly, perhaps she could work her way round to it somehow.

'Have you contacted his secretary yet to confirm your place on Monday's list?' she asked, certain that everything was connected in some way to the surgery.

'No,' he growled.

'Why not?' If he thought his surly expression was going to deflect her, he had another think coming.

'My body, my decision.' It was more of a snarl this time, but she could sense that it held more of the wounded animal about it than a threat, no matter what he'd intended.

'Of course,' she agreed lightly. 'And knowing

that you're someone who's undergone rigorous military training and has probably spent time he can't talk about in innumerable hell-holes, it couldn't possibly be fear that's preventing you from going under the knife again...or perhaps it is? Perhaps you don't trust even someone as good as Rick d'Agostino?'

'No! It's not that I don't trust him!' he exclaimed immediately, and she was relieved that she'd been able to sting him into delivering a whole sentence.

'Well, if it isn't that, what *is* it?' she demanded. 'Is it just that you don't want to talk about it with me because you've decided I don't have the right to know any more? Have you decided that you want a divorce after all?'

'No!' If anything, the response was even more emphatic this time, but then she saw an unexpectedly uncertain expression seep into his eyes. 'Unless that's what *you* want?'

'Of course I don't,' she said impatiently. 'If I'd wanted a divorce, I certainly wouldn't have shared a bed with you, or my body.' She was tempted to shriek with frustration, wondering how such a clever man could be so dense. Only the fact that it would upset the people staying in the rooms around them made her hang on to her control.

'Gregor, I think I fell in love with you the first day we met and I was devastated when I was told you'd died, but unless we can clear the air between us...unless we can start talking to each other and sharing our thoughts and feelings...we won't stand a chance of—'

'Face facts, Livvy,' he interrupted grimly. 'With me in a chair we don't stand much chance anyway. I'm not the person you married any more, so all the plans we'd made—'

'Neither of us is the same person.' It was her turn to butt in. 'Yes, you've been changed by what's happened to you—and I *don't* just mean the obvious physical changes—but I've changed too. The things that have happened to me over the last two years...believing that I'd lost you...then losing your b—'

She screeched to a halt but it was already too late.

She could feel the colour draining from her face as those liquid-silver eyes watched, their intent gaze telling her that his far-too-sharp brain was already dissecting all the possible endings to that sentence.

'You were pregnant?' he whispered with such certainty that it wasn't really a question. 'You were carrying our baby when I left?' Horror mixed with sadness and was followed closely by anger. 'Why didn't you tell me? Why did you keep it a secret? How far—?' He stopped himself and shook his head. 'What does it matter, now, how far along you were?' he exclaimed heatedly. 'What happened to the baby?'

'I don't know exactly how many weeks pregnant I was because it was accidental,' she said, deliberately starting at the beginning. 'We'd decided we wouldn't start our family until the end of your time on active service in the unit, but…possibly it happened during that clostridium outbreak when our shifts got changed around at short notice. I vaguely remember having to take a couple of my Pills later than I should…' And she wouldn't have remembered *that* much if she hadn't gone over and over it obsessively in the dark days after she'd lost everything that mattered to her.

'Once I'd taken the test, I was only waiting for you to get in contact with me, and if you were able to tell me that you'd been sent somewhere relatively safe, I would have…but the next thing I knew…' She could barely see him for the tears and her throat was so tight that she had to force the words out to finish the telling.

'They sent two of them, all dressed up in their best uniforms—as if that would somehow make it better—to inform me that you'd been killed in an explosion and that they couldn't even find enough of you to bring home for me to bury… just…just your mangled ID tags. That's…' She had to pause to draw in a shuddering breath, only then realising that she was sobbing as she spoke and that tears were streaming down her face.

She'd been harbouring the secret too long and it had been festering inside her ever since the moment she'd realised she couldn't even tell her mother about her dreadful loss, convinced that all she would receive were expressions of relief that there would be no permanent reminder of her 'ill-advised' marriage, rather than the sympathy she'd needed for losing the last precious part of the man she loved.

This man, she thought as she ran despairing eyes over him, trying to imagine, as she had so many times before, which parts of him their child would have inherited…his thick dark hair with its unruly tendency to curl, the strangely liquid quality to those silvery-grey eyes, or perhaps the lean, almost aristocratic profile and high cheekbones?

She tried to draw in a steadying breath to continue speaking but the pain of loss was too great for anything more than one last broken statement. '*That's* when I l-lost the b-baby.'

Gregor had never felt so helpless, trapped in a wheelchair by his useless legs when Livvy needed him to be able to take her in his arms, to cradle her against his heart and share her sorrow for the child they'd lost.

'Oh, Livvy, I'm so sorry,' he whispered. 'So sorry I wasn't there for you…so sorry you had to go through all that alone…' He tasted salt on his lips and realised that he was crying, too.

That was something he couldn't remember doing for many a long year but, then, he'd never before learned that he'd lost what might be the only chance he would ever have of a family.

His heart clenched inside his chest, and he finally understood the agony of all those people he'd seen in countries all around the world, trying to cope with similar losses.

Somewhere in the depths of his mind, images flickered of children screaming, surrounded by all the chaos of explosions and gunfire, and something told him that these faces were significant in some way to his own life. He tried to focus on them, hoping for recognition, but there was too much else going on inside his head at the moment.

He tried to wipe away the evidence of his unmanly weakness on a raised shoulder, but the tears kept coming as he mourned not just the death of their baby but everything this lovely woman had endured in the last two years.

Then, too, there was the inescapable fact that in his present condition there was so little he could do to make the future any better for her than the past.

There was little chance that he would be able to secure a job that would fulfil both his financial and emotional needs, and the prospect of spending the rest of his life doing little more than suturing lacerations was not enticing.

Perhaps he should look further into the possibilities of returning to his own country? Half a doctor would be better than none, until their medical services finally returned to normal, and he was certain that Lena and Mariska would welcome him with open arms.

Then there was the question that had haunted him since his teens…the fact that he'd never been able to bring himself to return to the place where his family was buried to tell them how sorry he was for letting them down.

But they were problems for another day.

Now all that mattered was giving Livvy the comfort she needed while his soul soaked up the solace she offered like a desert absorbing life-giving rain at the end of an interminable drought.

'I knew you'd been holding something back…' he mused in the darkness, and she realised she could hear the rumble of his words in the broad naked chest under her ear, too.

'Ever since I turned up at the church and you agreed to let me go back to the flat, I knew there was something you weren't telling me,' he continued, 'but I had no idea what it was.' He gave a soft growl of exasperation.

'I'd been going over and over it, trying to work it out. Was it the fact that I'd prevented you from marrying Ash? Was it the fact that I'm injured and don't know how much I'm going to improve? Perhaps you'd decided that you no longer loved me and were trying to find a way to break it to me that you wanted to go ahead with a divorce? But then you told me about your arrangement with Ash and you've explained that you were only getting the lawyer to check on the legality of our marriage after I'd been declared dead, and I was just left wondering if you were dreading having to care for a paraplegic for the rest of his life and—'

'No!' The relief she felt at having finally told him about the baby was almost overwhelmed by her guilt in delaying the telling.

To think that he'd been going over and over things in his head like that, believing that she was seeing him as an unwelcome burden when nothing could be further from the truth. 'Gregor, if you decide not to have surgery, I'd be unhappy...but only because I'm hoping Rick d'Agostino is going to be able to take some of the pain away.' She huffed out an exasperated breath. 'I know you hate being dependent on anyone or anything…and that includes pain-killers. But if you think that you being in a wheel-chair makes any difference to how I feel about you…well, you're an idiot!'

'But at least I'm a fully functioning idiot, even if I'm in a wheelchair,' he snapped, the mixture of anger and misery suddenly clear in his voice.

Suddenly, with her brain working at lightning speed to untangle the relevance of that single sentence, Olivia knew they'd finally reached the heart of the problem.

'That's what he told you?' she asked while everything inside her clenched tight in sympathy with his desolation. 'Rick said that if he operates, he can give you back your legs but you'll be unable to perform sexually?'

'It's a serious possibility,' he admitted, 'and knowing how much you've always wanted children…and especially now that I know you've already lost one…it just wouldn't be fair for—'

'Whoever told you life was going to be fair?' she interrupted heatedly. 'You know better than most that bad things happen to good people, too. And anyway,' she added quickly, preventing him

from butting in, 'having sex isn't the only way
of having babies, any more than it's the only
way of showing you love someone or of finding
fulfilment with them. So you certainly can't use
that as an excuse for pushing me away…unless
you don't love me any more and want that
divorce after all.'

Her heart was in her mouth as the challenging
words seemed to echo in the compact little suite
and time seemed to stretch into infinity as she
waited for his reply.

'Will you pass me the phone, please?' he asked
softly, and she blinked, suddenly wishing there
was more light in the room so that she could see
his expression.

'The phone?' Automatically, she reached out to
the bedside table for it and passed it to him, but
instead of taking it from her he wrapped long
lean fingers around her hand and tightened his
other arm around her to pull her closer.

'Well, assuming you meant what you said, I'm
going to need it to phone Rick d'Agostino's secretary to leave a message to put my name down
for that theatre slot.'

'So, does that mean you don't want a divorce?'

she challenged in a distinctly wobbly voice as she realised that it felt as if he never intended letting her go.

'I never did,' he said, 'but I still can't bear the thought of you being stuck with someone who can't—'

The only way she could think to stop him voicing any sort of doubt was to press her lips to his and rely on the combustive nature of their kisses to empty his mind of anything but their need for each other.

'We'll deal with it,' she whispered when they surfaced some time later, both of them breathless and already well on the way to naked. 'Whatever happens to you…to us…we'll find a way to deal with it, together.'

CHAPTER TEN

'THE operation's over, Gregor,' he heard Livvy say reassuringly, then felt the soft press of a kiss on his cheek. He couldn't even force his eyelids open, let alone move, although he tried, the effort wringing a hoarse groan out of him.

He had a vague memory of Rick d'Agostino telling him how pleased he was with the way the complex operation had gone, or had that just been wishful thinking while he had still been under the influence of the anaesthetic?

And he couldn't even summon up the words to ask.

One thing he was determined to do was open his eyes to catch his first glimpse of Livvy's face. One glimpse would be all he needed to know whether the surgery had been a success or not…to know whether he was going to have to leave her to find a man who *could* give her the family she wanted, while he spent the rest of his life reliving the images stored in his memory.

And even if the operation *had* been a success, that was only the first part of the battle to become something resembling his former self. At the moment, he knew there would be tubes and wires galore snaking to and from the drains and monitors connected to his body. Then there was the fact that he'd needed bone harvested from other sites on his body as well as donated cadaverous tissue to rebuild his damaged legs, pelvis and spine, so he had numerous surgical sites needing analgesia to dampen the pain while they healed. And that was all apart from the necessity of spending who knew how long facedown to allow the major incisions on his back to begin healing.

And it wasn't as if waiting for bone, muscle and skin to heal after the surgery was going to be the end of the story either. As he knew from his previous operations, there would be months of gruelling physiotherapy to build up his wasted muscles and restore their function, and all of that would have to happen before he could even start to put weight on his legs to see if he could once again use them for walking.

And he still didn't know if that was going to be possible, this time, any more than the last.

Finally he managed to force his eyelids open just a crack.

The light in the room seemed almost painfully bright and it took him several seconds before he could focus on Livvy's face…and his heart nearly stopped when he saw the tears sliding steadily down her cheeks to drip off her chin.

Livvy was crying.

She was sitting at his bedside, crying.

That must mean that the operation had been a failure—but in what way?

Did her tears mean that he still wouldn't be able to walk…wouldn't be able to go back to the sort of medicine that left him satisfied at the end of a day, no matter how gory or how mundane the cases had been? Or did it mean that Rick d'Agostino had been forced to tell her that her husband would never be able to make love to her again?

His crushing disappointment must have forced a sound out of him because suddenly she looked up from the hand she was holding to see that he was awake and looking at her…and she smiled.

It was the smile he'd seen in his dreams for two long years; the smile that had saved him from going mad when he'd had no idea who *he* was, let alone who *she* was…

'Oh, Gregor,' she whispered, more tears brimming in her eyes. 'It went well. *Everything* went well.' And he suddenly realised that, in spite of the tears, her eyes were glittering with happiness. 'Obviously, you're going to have to do a *bit* of work to get fit before I'll be able to send you back to work…'

They shared a wry grin at the irony in her choice of word because they both knew just how many gruelling months of effort it was really going to take, but at this moment he didn't care about that. All he could think about was the fact that there was still a chance that he could keep Livvy in his life, forever…or at least until he knew whether there had been any collateral damage done during the operation. There would be plenty of time to contemplate a life without her if he discovered that he could no longer give her the family she deserved.

'What's the matter?' Livvy demanded. 'Are you in pain? Does your analgesia need topping up?'

'Why would you think I'm in pain?' he asked, his words distorted by his position while he silently kicked himself for not controlling his expression better.

Livvy snorted derisively. 'Firstly, because I'm a qualified doctor and well-accustomed to reading patients' faces, and, secondly, because I've known you long enough to be able to tell when you're thinking or feeling something and you're trying to hide it from me. So, don't think you can pull the wool over my eyes by turning my question back at me. If you're in pain, I need you to tell me. If it's a worry of any other sort, I need to know that, too.'

Such a determined tone of voice was the best antidote to anaesthetic hangover he knew. Where before he'd been having difficulty keeping his eyes open, now he was wide awake and all-too aware of the concern she was feeling.

Suddenly, he knew that it wouldn't be fair to leave the situation hanging for however many days or weeks it might be until he knew how complete his recovery was going to be. They had always been equal partners in their relationship and it would not be right to allow Livvy to think that everything had been solved when their marriage could be ending in the near future.

'Did...did d'Agostino say anything about... about collateral damage?' he asked in a voice that, even to his own ears, sounded as if it had emerged over a mile of gravel track.

'Collateral damage?' she repeated with a frown before the penny dropped and the wash of heat that appeared in her cheeks was the most spectacular blush he'd seen since he'd reappeared in her life.

'Well,' she said after a pause that seemed eons long before she spoke again, 'he did say that the extent of the damage was less than he'd feared, so the operative field was more contained than he'd expected...but he wasn't able to give me any idea how long we'd have to leave it before we can start experimenting,' she finished, completely robbing him of what little breath he had left.

'That's enough of that talk, Olivia Davidson!' exclaimed a voice with a pronounced Mediterranean accent from the doorway as the surgeon in question came into the room. 'At least you could give the poor man time to get over the anaesthetic before you start talking about having your wicked way with him!' Then it was Gregor's turn to feel the heat sweep up his throat and into his face in a scalding tide. He was actually grateful that he was lying face-down in the bed so that his embarrassment was largely hidden.

It seemed like hours later before both the surgeon and the anaesthetist had pronounced themselves satisfied with Gregor's initial recovery from the surgery so that he could be transferred out of Post-Op, then there seemed to be dozens of minor delays before he could be ensconced in the ultra-swish surroundings of a private room.

Not that it was just any private room. The hospital had made a financial decision to cater for some of the wealthier international patients who needed to take advantage of the fact that the hospital was a centre of excellence.

It had been Rick d'Agostino's decision that his patient should be transferred into one of those individual high-dependency rooms, to give a fellow member of staff a much-needed degree of privacy, but the hospital grapevine was probably already alive with rumours. Perhaps they imagined that there was royalty or a reclusive rock-star in residence?

Gregor had slept through most of the turmoil, leaving Olivia free to think while she gazed her fill at what she could see of the lean planes of his face, so pale against those thick dark lashes and hair. The light caught several silvery strands at his temples, but that was hardly surprising after the stresses of the last two years.

As ever, his torso above the crisp white sheet was naked, and if she ignored the stark white dressings over the single operation site she could see, she could concentrate on admiring the amazingly well-muscled breadth of his shoulders. In fact, she was looking forward to exploring his whole body as soon as he was fit enough, with all the time in the world to investigate and reacquaint herself with the man she loved.

Suddenly she was brought to the edge of tears by the thought that she had come so close to losing him forever; that she might never have seen him again if it weren't for sheer luck and the dedication of those two women who'd nursed him.

But mostly she was thinking about what Gregor's unguarded face had revealed in that first conversation as he'd been emerging from the anaesthetic.

She had no doubt that, in spite of what she'd said, if the operation had gone badly he'd still had every intention of walking away from their marriage to allow her to find a man who could give her the family they'd planned.

It was just the sort of unselfish thing that Gregor would do. He was the product of a childhood in which he'd had everything stripped away from him in the blink of an eye, and now he automatically reacted by finding ways to help others in similar situations, even if it meant putting his own life in danger.

This time, though, she didn't know whether to admire his impulse toward self-sacrifice or berate him for it. As if finding someone else to be the father of her children could ever be a simple matter of substituting one sperm donor for another!

Those thoughts were uppermost in her mind

when he finally opened his eyes again, their liquid-silver depths gleaming at her in obvious delight when he saw her sitting at his bedside.

'It wouldn't have mattered, you know,' she blurted, almost startling herself as the words burst out of her involuntarily. 'We'd have found a way.'

'W-what wouldn't have mattered?' His voice sounded almost rusty and he was as adorably rumpled-looking as if he'd woken up beside her after a long night of love-making.

'If it had turned out that you couldn't... perform,' she offered, and could have kicked herself for using such a ghastly euphemism when she was a medical professional with all the correct terminology at her disposal. All she could do was ignore her self-inflicted embarrassment and plough on, the words almost a gabble, they emerged so fast.

'It's not as if there's only one way for us to satisfy each other or show our love and...and if we decided we wanted to go down that route, we could opt for semen collection so I could get pregnant. In fact, if we'd thought of it sooner, we could have collected some and had it frozen before you had your—'

'I did, Livvy,' he interrupted, stopping her in her tracks.

'W-when?' she croaked. 'You only knew three days ago that you were having surgery, so—'

'The process doesn't take very long,' he pointed out with a teasing grin, then crooked his finger and beckoned her closer, wrapping long lean fingers around her hand to pull her closer still until she had to lean against the side of the bed, her face almost as close as if they were sharing the pillow.

'I have a confession to make,' he murmured as he distracted her by stroking his thumb over her knuckles. 'I knew, logically, that I shouldn't be selfish…shouldn't tie you to me if everything went wrong…should set you free to find someone to give you the babies you wanted…' He closed his eyes briefly and shook his head. 'But I also wanted to be prepared…to have all the ammunition ready to fight for you…to persuade you that *I* could give you those babies even if they couldn't be conceived in the normal way…'

'Oh, Gregor…' she breathed, touched beyond belief, and had to battle with the hot threat of tears.

She angled her head to press a cautious kiss to

the corner of his mouth. 'Surely you know by now that the only babies I would want are yours, no matter how we have them. And even if we could *never* have children, you're still the only husband I want; the only man who'll ever share my bed and my heart.'

The brief tap at the door was almost welcome, cutting through the turbulent emotions that threatened to overwhelm her, and the nurse who came in to take Gregor's vital signs gave her time to remember some of the questions that had plagued her while she'd waited those interminable hours for the surgery to be over.

'Tell me about Oksana,' she invited when they were alone again.

'Which one?' he countered, and she blinked.

'I didn't know there were two,' she said. 'Which one was in your nightmare?'

'Both of them, probably,' he admitted grimly, then told her of the young girl he'd rescued from the cellar who had survived both artillery shelling and an exploding boiler with little more than scratches and bruises.

'And the other one?' Olivia prompted eagerly,

glad that Gregor's sacrifice had resulted in such
a successful outcome.

'She was my sister,' he said, and his sombre
tone told her that this story didn't have a happy
ending.

It was several minutes before he continued and
the pain in his eyes almost made her regret
asking, but finally he began.

'It was the school holidays and because our
parents both went out to work, it was my job to
take care of Oksana and Janek and keep them
safe because I was the eldest. Then my parents
were killed while they were queuing for bread
and sausages, and there was only me to look
after them. Then the explosions came closer and
closer to our apartment building and I was so
sure that the only safe place was down in the
cellar...but then the walls collapsed and when
the neighbours came to help, I was the only one
they found alive and the authorities sent me to
an orphanage.'

'Oh, Gregor...' Her heart ached so badly for
everything he'd been through...not once, but
twice. She was sorry she'd made him relive such
a harrowing experience but glad that he'd told

her because it explained so much about the man he'd become.

'Will you come with me?' he demanded suddenly, leaving her nonplussed.

'Come where?'

'To my home town to find their graves. Maybe the nightmares will go away if I can tell them I'm sorry that I didn't—'

The brisk tap at the door interrupted him, then the unit's senior sister stuck her neatly-styled head around it. 'I'm sorry to interrupt, but there's a Lieutenant-Colonel on the phone for Mr… Dr…Captain…' Olivia had to chuckle at the poor woman's flustered stumbling over the correct form of Gregor's name.

'It will probably be easier if you just call him Gregor,' she suggested, before she turned to the man lying unusually silently beside her. 'I presume he's one of your superiors. Do you feel up to speaking to him or shall I take a message?'

'You might as well,' he said. 'He's a good senior officer—cares about his men. He's probably only checking up on me to make sure I survived the surgery.'

Except that wasn't anything like the message

that Olivia was given to pass on, and when she hung up the phone it took her several seconds to catch her breath.

'What was all that about?' Gregor demanded impatiently, and stirred her out of her shock.

'He said your unit was contacted by someone from the embassy. Apparently, the nursing staff you worked with and the villagers whose children you saved from the explosion have been making enquiries of all their friends and relations.' She smiled briefly at the similarities between such a close-knit community and the hospital grapevine she'd been thinking about just a little while ago.

'He said that it's taken a while because so much of the communications infrastructure was damaged during the fighting, but one thing led to another and…' She paused to grip his hand tightly. 'Gregor, they think they've tracked down some surviving members of your family!'

'What?' he gasped, then groaned when he tried to shake his head too violently. 'That's impossible! There was no-one left…no-one at all. I didn't manage to save any of them…my parents, my brother, my sister…they were all gone.'

'Didn't you just tell me they were called Janek and Oksana?'

'Yes, but—'

Olivia had one eye on the monitor that was recording his blood pressure and pulse, wondering if this was the wrong time to be having this whole conversation. But how could she *not* tell him when it was such good news?

'The embassy just informed your Lieutenant-Colonel that there are a Janek and an Oksana Davidov who have believed, ever since they were children, that their big brother Gregor was killed while saving their lives.'

The next few hours were full of frustration for Olivia as she waited for all the necessary strings to be pulled; hours of watching Gregor fret at the delay even as he tried to school himself to expect disappointment.

Finally, without any sign of the fanfare that the momentous call deserved, the phone rang and she handed it to Gregor.

'*Da. Etta Gregor Davidov,*' he said in a voice made guttural by tension, his knuckles bone-white as he gripped the plastic so tightly that she was afraid it would shatter in his hand.

She couldn't hear what the voice on the other end said, but she didn't need to, not when she could see the tears of joy gather in Gregor's eyes and the tremulous smile that began at the corners of his mouth and grew until it filled his whole face.

'*Janek*?' he whispered in disbelief. '*Etta Janek*?'

He looked across at her and held his hand out to beckon her closer, wanting to share with her the delight of hearing his brother's voice for the first time in so very many years, and her heart overflowed with the soul-deep realisation that she loved this man with every fibre of her being and would love him for the rest of her life.

'*Yalki palki!*' panted the young woman as she sweated her way through the last series of repetitions under the supervision of the physiotherapist. '*Starrest ni radest!*' she shouted at the end, swiping at the rivulets of sweat beading her face and throat.

'You didn't actually teach Sherilee to swear!' Livvy demanded in a hushed whisper, clearly horrified.

'I promised I would, so I had to keep my word,' Gregor said piously, then spoilt it by grinning at her. 'I just hope I'm not anywhere in the vicinity if she feels the need to swear at someone from my country. If they fall about laughing and tell her what she's actually saying…'

'So, what *did* you teach her?' Livvy demanded, clearly intrigued. 'What does *yalki palki* mean?'

'*Yalki* is Christmas tree,' he explained, 'and *palki* is the tree after Christmas, when all the needles have fallen off.'

'But if it's said with the right degree of venom…like someone saying *sugar* instead of using a less socially acceptable word… So, what about the other thing she said? *Starrest* something?'

'You have a good ear for the language,' he complimented her. 'Perhaps I should have thought about teaching you before now, when we're about to fly out there. At least you would have been able to greet some of the older people who haven't had a chance to learn any English.'

'Perhaps we'll have time for a crash course on the flight,' she suggested. 'But don't think you've sidetracked me. What *was* that other phrase?'

'*Starrest ni radest?*' he repeated, making certain to accentuate the guttural roll of the words, knowing full well the visceral effect it had on her. 'That's one I've been saying fairly often myself while I've been getting these damn legs working again. It means "growing old is no fun" but whatever you do, don't tell Sherilee.'

The young woman in question was making her way over to them, a slender, glowing picture of health who looked as if she'd never had a day's illness in her life.

'So, doctor big-shot, who won the race?' she challenged with a grin.

'Well, you've been signed off fit to go dancing tonight, and I've officially handed in my wheel-chair for good, so how about we call it a tie?' he suggested.

The brave young woman knew she would have to come back into hospital later in the year for a further operation to have some of the metalwork 'scaffolding' removed from around her spine, but the way her body had healed already after coming so close to paraplegia was amazing.

'I suppose so,' Sherilee conceded. 'You said you might have to invest in a really trendy walking stick—like that Dr House on TV—and I'll probably never be quite as flexible as I once was but, hey, nobody ever promised that getting older was going to be a picnic.'

Gregor smiled at Livvy over Sherilee's head as the youngster hugged him, sharing with her the irony that the young woman had paraphrased the words he'd taught her all those weeks ago when they had both been in the early stages of their rehabilitation.

Livvy threw a meaningful glance towards the large clock on the far wall, reminding him that they really didn't have time to linger. This meeting had been squeezed in when Sherilee had told him that she was coming in for her last physio session, so that he could congratulate her in person. The two of them had formed an unexpectedly close alliance during their rehab, alternately egging each other on and vying with each other to make the greatest progress and commiserating when improvement was slow and depression threatened.

'Hey, you two don't have time to hang around here!' Sherilee exclaimed suddenly. 'You've got a plane to catch, haven't you? You're off to visit your family so you can pick up some new swear words.'

'Something like that,' he agreed as he gave

her shoulder a farewell pat. 'Enjoy your dancing tonight.'

'Send me a postcard?'

'I'll send one to the physio department,' Gregor said, and winked at her. 'Now that you're not a patient any more, you'll have to ask one of the physios to let you see the card.' The wash of pink in her cheeks told him he hadn't mistaken her interest in one of the newest members of staff. He'd told Livvy of his suspicions that Sherilee's new-found determination to become a physio-therapist herself had begun when the handsome young man had started work in the department.

'Ready to go?' Livvy asked with the lilt of laughter in her voice, and all thoughts of other people's budding romances were banished.

'With you? Anywhere,' he agreed as he held his elbow out for her to slip her hand through it. The manoeuvre was their own personal com-promise and had been Livvy's suggestion, knowing just how much he'd hated being depen-dent on mechanical aids for so long.

He wasn't completely recovered from the re-constructive surgery, and should really have been using at least one stick for stability and safety, but with Livvy by his side, providing physical support as well as all the emotional and psychological sustenance he could ever want, he'd decided that their trip couldn't wait any longer.

'Then there's a reunion we need to get to…one that's years overdue,' he said, hearing the husky tone in his own voice and unashamed of it. To have learned after so many lonely years that some of his family had survived those terrible days and were even now waiting to welcome him home…it was hardly surprising that he'd broken down after that first phone call and wept in Livvy's arms.

And he had a feeling he would be weeping again when he proudly introduced his wife to them and told them that the next generation of Davidovs was already on its way.

He glanced down at the barely-there curve of her slender body, still unable to believe how much everything had changed for the better since he'd had Livvy back in his life. 'We've been so lucky,' he whispered, the soft words almost lost under the growl of traffic around them.

As if she was reading his mind, Livvy stroked

one hand over the just-visible evidence of the pregnancy and leant her head on his shoulder to say, 'It really wouldn't have mattered, you know…if we hadn't been able to have this without some form of medical intervention. I still wouldn't have let you use it as an excuse to get rid of me.'

'Get rid of you?' he exclaimed, stung by the suggestion. 'That wasn't what I wanted to do. If I hadn't been able to…' He shook his head. 'I just wanted you to be able to have the family you deserve, and if that meant I had to let you go…to let you find a man who could give you those babies…'

'Well, I hope you understand now…that there wouldn't…*couldn't* have been any babies without you,' she said fiercely. '*You* are the heart of my family. Without you there wouldn't be any point. The babies are just…just a by-product—a very welcome by-product, I agree,' she said hastily when he would have interrupted, 'but they could never be more important to me than having you in my life.'

'I hope you still feel that way when you find out what's waiting for us when we get to the end of our journey. Janek and Oksana have been notifying even the most distant family member they can find, and it sounds as if they've been organising a gathering for the official wedding reception we would have had if we'd married in my home.'

'Official wedding reception?' She frowned as she looked up at him. 'What do you mean? Gregor, everything's already been sorted out now that your death has been struck off the records.'

'I know that, but apparently the official wedding reception is what the old people are calling it.' He shrugged. 'Of course, so much has changed in the last twenty-five or thirty years. Titles and estates aren't as important these days the way they were centuries ago when—'

'Hang on a minute,' she interrupted. 'What do you mean, titles and estates? You're not telling me that you come from a family of wealthy landowners?'

'Well, I don't know about wealthy,' he said diffidently, 'nor do I know whether there's still any land involved, and as for titles…in a country that had communism imposed on it for so long, such things really don't have much place…'

She started to chuckle and his words died away.

'What?' he demanded, slightly taken-aback by her reaction.

'I'm sorry, Gregor, but don't you see the funny side of this?' she asked through rising gales of merriment. 'My mother has spent years looking down her nose at you, wishing I'd married into the titled family nextdoor instead. I can't imagine what her reaction will be if she ever finds out that she's had the son-in-law of her dreams right under her nose all the time.'

'I imagine even your mother might be impressed if she saw that map,' he agreed. 'Do you remember the one Janek emailed, in with all those historic documents that showed the region my family came from?'

'The one with that red outline on it?' she asked. 'I thought that was the equivalent of the parish boundary around the houses and fields where you lived?'

'Actually, they were whole villages that were once full of the people who worked the land around there…the land that was once owned by my family.' He raised a dark brow, uncertain for a moment exactly what she was thinking. 'I'm sorry if you're disappointed that any titles there are left don't come with any vast estates.'

'I'm not disappointed at all,' she reassured him. 'I'm quite happy with the man I married straight out of medical school. He's a dedicated doctor, a committed humanitarian, a wonderful husband…'

'A spectacular lover,' he prompted.

'That goes without saying,' she agreed with a grin, 'especially since you seem determined to make up for all the time we lost.'

They shared heated glances and he reached up to cup her cheek. 'It's a shame we have to check in at the airport so early, only to wait around for hours. I can think of other, far more pleasurable things we could be doing rather than wasting time.'

'Hold that thought,' she murmured as the taxi drew up outside the terminal at the start of their long-awaited journey. 'But remember, Gregor, we've got all the time in the world now. We've been given a second chance and not one minute of it will be wasted all the while we have each other.'

MEDICAL™

Large Print

Titles for the next six months...

December

THE MIDWIFE AND THE MILLIONAIRE	Fiona McArthur
FROM SINGLE MUM TO LADY	Judy Campbell
KNIGHT ON THE CHILDREN'S WARD	Carol Marinelli
CHILDREN'S DOCTOR, SHY NURSE	Molly Evans
HAWAIIAN SUNSET, DREAM PROPOSAL	Joanna Neil
RESCUED: MOTHER AND BABY	Anne Fraser

January

DARE SHE DATE THE DREAMY DOC?	Sarah Morgan
DR DROP-DEAD GORGEOUS	Emily Forbes
HER BROODING ITALIAN SURGEON	Fiona Lowe
A FATHER FOR BABY ROSE	Margaret Barker
NEUROSURGEON...AND MUM!	Kate Hardy
WEDDING IN DARLING DOWNS	Leah Martyn

February

WISHING FOR A MIRACLE	Alison Roberts
THE MARRY-ME WISH	Alison Roberts
PRINCE CHARMING OF HARLEY STREET	Anne Fraser
THE HEART DOCTOR AND THE BABY	Lynne Marshall
THE SECRET DOCTOR	Joanna Neil
THE DOCTOR'S DOUBLE TROUBLE	Lucy Clark

 MILLS & BOON®

MEDICAL™

Large Print

March

DATING THE MILLIONAIRE DOCTOR	Marion Lennox
ALESSANDRO AND THE CHEERY NANNY	Amy Andrews
VALENTINO'S PREGNANCY BOMBSHELL	Amy Andrews
A KNIGHT FOR NURSE HART	Laura Iding
A NURSE TO TAME THE PLAYBOY	Maggie Kingsley
VILLAGE MIDWIFE, BLUSHING BRIDE	Gill Sanderson

April

BACHELOR OF THE BABY WARD	Meredith Webber
FAIRYTALE ON THE CHILDREN'S WARD	Meredith Webber
PLAYBOY UNDER THE MISTLETOE	Joanna Neil
OFFICER, SURGEON…GENTLEMAN!	Janice Lynn
MIDWIFE IN THE FAMILY WAY	Fiona McArthur
THEIR MARRIAGE MIRACLE	Sue MacKay

May

DR ZINETTI'S SNOWKISSED BRIDE	Sarah Morgan
THE CHRISTMAS BABY BUMP	Lynne Marshall
CHRISTMAS IN BLUEBELL COVE	Abigail Gordon
THE VILLAGE NURSE'S HAPPY-EVER-AFTER	Abigail Gordon
THE MOST MAGICAL GIFT OF ALL	Fiona Lowe
CHRISTMAS MIRACLE: A FAMILY	Dianne Drake

MILLS & BOON®